D1013094

LILY'S
MOUNTAIN

LILY'S MOUNTAIN

by Hannah Moderow

HOUGHTON MIFFLIN HARCOURT
Boston New York

www.hmhco.com

The text was set in Adobe Jenson Pro.

Library of Congress Cataloging-in-Publication Data
Names: Moderow, Hannah, author.
Title: Lily's mountain / written by Hannah Moderow.
Description: Boston ; New York : Houghton Mifflin Harcourt, [2017] |
Summary: Unable to believe their father died while climbing Mount Denali,
twelve-year-old Lily and her older sister, Sophie, climb the mountain
in order to rescue him.
Identifiers: LCCN 2016037231 | ISBN 9780544978003 (hardcover)
Subjects: | CYAC: Mountaineering — Fiction. | Fathers and daughters — Fiction.
| Sisters — Fiction. | Family life — Alaska — Fiction. | Denali, Mount (Alaska) —
Fiction. | Alaska — Fiction.
Classification: LCC PZ7.1.M6368 Lil 2017 | DDC [Fic] — dc23
LC record available at https://lccn.loc.gov/2016037231

Manufactured in the United States of America
DOC 10 9 8 7 6 5 4 3 2 1
4500678628

33614080597072

For Mom, Dad, and Andy — with love.

With gratitude to the wise mentors
and writing teachers of my life.

Finally, to Erik and Matilda — adventures await!

CHAPTER 1

Dad left three and a half weeks ago with a mug of coffee, a box of chocolate-glazed donuts, and a backpack with everything he needed to climb Denali. Before he left, he pulled me into a bear hug and said, "See you after I touch my toes to the summit."

"You bet," I told him, already eager for his return.

As Dad backed out of the driveway, I waved from the porch, wishing more than anything that I could hop into his truck and tag along. Climbing mountains is the surest way to kiss the sky and sleep close to the stars. And Dad always said that from the top of Denali he could taste a little bit of heaven.

Dad touched his toes to the summit, all right. His climbing partner, John, told us he did it on a no-breeze, blue-sky day.

1

But something happened on the way down.

The phone rang yesterday while I was making Dad's welcome-home brownies. Sophie and I raced each other through the kitchen to answer it, but Mom beat us there.

"Hello," she said, her eyes lit up with expectation. Sophie and I stood side by side, watching for Mom's big smile at the sound of Dad's voice. But the smile never came. Just weird silence, and then her hands started shaking — hard.

"Are you sure?" she asked, and she took in a really deep breath and held it. She nodded slowly, and when she finally let out her breath, she said, "No, no, *no!*" Each "no" was louder than the one before. She clicked the phone off and staggered through the back door and onto the porch. She slumped over the railing with her head in her hands.

I chased after her. "What is it? What is it?" I asked as my face got hot and my body started shivering even though it was warm and sunny outside.

Mom lifted her head from her hands and said, "He's gone." She paced back and forth along the porch before sitting on the edge of the flower box that Dad had built in time for Mother's Day this year.

"What do you mean, 'gone'?" Sophie asked, standing in the doorway.

"He fell in a crevasse, and they can't find him."

"Well, they must not be looking hard enough," I said. It didn't make sense: Dad knew everything about crevasses, and he knew exactly how to rescue himself if he fell inside one.

"Was he roped up?" I asked.

"No," said Mom, but Dad *always* roped up on glaciers.

Mom continued, this time whispering: "They've tried everything. He's *gone*."

I shook my head. "No way."

Mom stood up from the flower box. Her eyes flashed with a panic I'd never seen before. "I told him not to climb that mountain again," she said. "I had a feeling that something would go wrong."

No! Denali was Dad's sacred mountain, and he'd climbed her six times before. Why would he have a problem now?

Sophie ran back into the house and didn't bother shutting the door. Her feet pounded up the staircase, almost as loud as the pounding in my head at the thought of Dad trapped anywhere.

"Mom, what can we do?" I asked.

She looked across the backyard to nowhere in particular and said one horrible word: "Nothing." Then she bowed her head like a wounded bird.

"We *have* to do something," I said. "I'm not giving up on Dad."

"Lily, sometimes the mountain wins."

"No!" I ran into the house and up the stairs. "Sophie, Sophie!" I called.

I found her in Mom and Dad's closet. She was pulling clothes to the floor just the way she taught me how to make a hide-and-seek spot when I was a little girl. She took Dad's blue flannel shirt off its hanger, and his gray woolly socks from the drawer, and his tan Carhartt pants that were folded on the shelf. She kept pulling clothes to the floor until the mound was high. Then she lay down and buried her face in the faded fabrics that smelled of Dad and campfires and adventures.

I collapsed too and buried my face in Dad's favorite blue flannel, but here's the thing: I knew better than to give up on Dad.

CHAPTER 2

Dad's been missing in the crevasse for just over two days. Long enough for the phone to ring and ring and ring. Long enough for Dad's climbing partner, John, to drop off some of his gear. Long enough for Mom to pace the house and for flowers to show up at the door. Long enough for Dad's outdoor column in the newspaper to show up empty. Well, not quite empty, but they plugged in a filler story about arctic ground squirrel hibernation because Dad wasn't home to meet his story deadline. And long enough for neighbors and friends to start hovering around.

The first time a knock comes to the door today, I answer it.

"I'm so sorry, honey," says Barb, Mom's church friend. She's holding a green bean casserole with pink polka-dotted oven mitts. Her face is warm and kind, but I can't take it — those fat tears sliding down her face.

Before I say anything, she walks right into the house. In a blink, Barb and I are in the kitchen alone. I don't know what to say. I often hike mountains with Dad while Mom's at church, and how do I respond to those fat tears?

"You know, Lily," Barb says, "Moses died on a mountain too."

I'm not sure which is worse: the tears or the green bean casserole or the thought of Moses dying.

"Dad's not dead," I say.

Barb looks at me with owly wide eyes like I'm a crazy person.

"He'll be back soon," I finish.

Mom walks in right then, and there's a silence as tall and icy as Denali. I slowly back out of the kitchen while Barb hugs Mom, and both of them have fat tears sliding down their faces.

Dad always heads for the garage when church ladies come over, so that's exactly what I do. I walk down the hallway and through the laundry room, and when I get to the garage, it's quiet and dark — a relief from all the light. It's almost never dark outside in the summer in Alaska, the land of the midnight sun.

I feel my way beyond the bikes and the ski rack to get to Dad's workbench. His secret candy stash is on the third shelf from the bottom.

I don't need light to be able to feel for a small bag of gummy bears. When I find one, I open it with my teeth and start eating.

One bear.

What happened?

Two bears.

How far did he fall?

Three bears.

Why wasn't he roped up?

Four bears.

I have to find him.

When I was really little, Dad lured me up mountains with gummy bears.

"I'll give you a red one if you make it to that scraggly spruce tree up there," he'd say, pointing. I'd think about that red gummy bear all the way to the tree and forget how tired my legs were. Once we reached the tree, Dad would hand over the bear and add a new goal: "I'll give you a red bear *and* a green bear if you make it to that rock." Yes, it was bribery, but it was fun, too. "Hell, if you make it all the way to the top, Lily, you can finish this bag of bears."

And I would.

I stuff a bunch of gummy bears in my mouth at once, and I hear Dad's words: "Lily — hope knocks the socks off fear."

So I eat gummy bears and hope. More gummy bears, more hope.

But I can't quite push away the smell of green bean casserole and the thought of Moses dying on a mountain.

CHAPTER 3

Dad digs his fingernails into the ice and crawls inch by inch out of the crevasse. When his head comes up into the light above the mountain, he slips and slides back down.

"Help," I scream, but nothing comes out. "Help!" I scream for real, and my own voice pulls me back into the world. I awake with a jolt from the nightmare.

It's 12:07 a.m. I blink my eyes open and shut, and then I remember: Dad is missing, Mom served me cold green bean casserole for dinner, and everything is wrong, wrong, wrong.

And the earth is shaking. The brass pulls on my dresser are actually rattling.

Earthquake!

The earth gets going. *Really* going. Zigging and zagging. The ground rumbles like a train.

I curl my knees up to my chest and clutch the bedpost. From my cocoon I see the framed photograph skid off the nightstand and crash to the floor. Glass shatters.

The earth stops just when I think it never will. Then Mom swings open my bedroom door.

"You okay, Lily?" she asks, her voice weary. She fidgets in the dim light.

"Fine," I say, and pull the comforter up to my chin, but nothing at all feels fine.

"Do you think Dad felt the quake?" I ask, a sudden vision of ice cracking.

"I don't know," Mom says. She stands statue-still in the doorway, like she has a lot to say but can't bring herself to get started.

"Maybe the glacier shifted in the quake, and Dad can climb out now," I say.

"I wish," Mom says. "How I wish." She lingers in the doorway for another few seconds. Then I hear her slippers pivot and scuffle down the hallway toward Sophie's room.

Mom must be thinking about Dad in the glacier during the earthquake too.

I sit up in bed. Then I see Dad: down on the floor, beneath the shattered glass. It's the photo of us standing at the top of Wolverine Peak.

"The best thing in the world is to stand on a mountaintop," Dad told me when we climbed Wolverine last month — the first big hike of early summer.

We sat at the top of the mountain on the flat ground beyond the jagged boulders. There we sipped our drinks — a can of Orange Crush for me and a mini flask of brandy for Dad. The city of Anchorage glimmered below us: little dot houses, line roads, and patches of brown turning to summery green. Three ravens circled overhead, twirling in the wind.

Most of the city was just waking up, but Dad and I had been climbing for hours. "Never waste the summer sun," he'd said when he woke me up that day. He had a newspaper deadline that night, but you never would have known it. He lived in the moment when he was in the mountains.

Sophie stayed home that day to get ready for senior prom. High school had officially zapped her love for the mountains. She was more interested in fruity lip gloss, tight blue jeans, parties, and some boy named Clint.

Mom didn't climb Wolverine with us either. She said she was meeting a friend for coffee, but I think she wanted to keep an eye on Sophie and her prom prep. Mom's a planner and an organizer. I'm more of a doer . . . just like Dad.

Mom and Sophie missed out. Sitting atop that mountain so early felt like finding the first lucky ladybug of summer.

"There she is," Dad said and pointed north.

Denali. From our perch on Wolverine, Denali did not look as tall as I knew she was: 20,310 feet. The snowy mountain sparkled under the clear blue sky.

"If I climb back up here when you're on Denali," I asked, "could I wave to you over there at the top of the world?"

"I might not be able to see you so far away," said Dad, "but I'm sure I'd know you were there." He grinned.

"How?" I asked.

Dad sipped his brandy before answering. "I think of it as mountain sense," he said. "Those of us who climb mountains know when others are climbing. We connect from the top."

"Can I climb Denali with you someday?" I asked.

"Yes. We'll climb her together."

"Promise?"

"Gummy bear promise," Dad said. He pulled a bag of bears from his backpack and dumped some of them into my hand. Then he took his own handful.

The promise was delicious — one white bear, four red ones, two yellow, and three green. I could almost taste my two feet on the top of Denali.

CHAPTER 4

As I lie awake, trying to get rid of the earthquake jitters, I think about what Mom said to Dad before he left for the mountain. "Charley, if you keep on climbing Denali, it will kill you eventually ... and then what?"

At the time, I thought Mom was being dramatic. Dad had been climbing for twenty years, so why would he stop now? What could go wrong *now*?

"You can't take the mountains out of me," Dad said. He assured Mom that this Denali trip would be his last big climb for a while. He had stories to write for the newspaper, he said, and camping trips to go on with all of us.

But I didn't quite believe him — that his big climbs would slow down. Dad could hardly stand a week without at least climbing Wolverine or another peak in the Chugach Range above Anchorage. Mom loves mountains too, but she doesn't trust them like Dad does. Doubt creeps in, and Mom can't push it away.

I'm starting to think Dad crawled out of the crevasse but he's afraid to come home — afraid that if he does, Mom will never let him climb another big mountain again. Here's the truth: Dad has to climb mountains, and so do I. It's what we do, and we're good at it.

Dad taught me how to hike up mountains before he even taught me the alphabet. I knew tundra underfoot before I knew how to scribble *A, B, C* on paper. He taught me what to wear to stay warm, and how to scrunch up my toes inside my boots in order to get a good grip on the earth.

Even though Sophie and Mom are in the house tonight, it's hard not to feel alone. Sophie told me to scram when I knocked on her door and tried to join her in her room.

Sophie's eighteen, six years older than me and ten times more dramatic. When things aren't to her liking, she stomps around and storms out of the house like a freshly lit sparkler that snaps and crackles all over the place. I can never quite tell her mood, but I like it when the *old* Sophie shows up occasionally — the sister who loves adventure.

Dad told me that Sophie's like a ptarmigan in springtime whose feathers are half-white from winter and half-brown for summer. "She's not sure what season it is," Dad said. "Don't worry; she'll move into her summer feathers soon."

I hope Dad's right.

Dad confronted Sophie the night before he left for the mountain. It had something to do with not giving her permission to go to a party. I didn't hear all of it, but the ordeal ended with Sophie yelling "I hate you," and she slammed the bedroom door in Dad's face.

Sophie's not an I-hate-you sort of girl, but now she's stuck with those parting words. *I. Hate. You.* Stuck with them until we find Dad. Then she can have another chance.

The brass handles clink against the bureau. I know what's coming.

The earth starts shaking — again. An aftershock!

"Stop," I say, and clutch the bedpost, but everything in my life is shaking, rattling, moving.

When the earth finally stills, Mom's feet don't come down the hallway. And there's no way I can sleep. Not tonight. Dad's alive, and he might only have a few days left.

I'm his last hope, and I have to come up with a plan.

I pull Dad's journal out from under my pillow and flip through the pages again. Dad's climbing partner, John, came by and left it with us yesterday. When he came, none of us asked what we all were wondering: Why hadn't Dad been roped up when he fell? Had he been reckless? I hoped his journal might answer some questions.

I asked John how he had Dad's journal. He told me he found it inside the tent pocket. Dad usually wrote his journal entries before bed, snuggled inside his sleeping bag, so he must have forgotten to put it in his pack the next morning.

I've already read Dad's journal twice and studied the map that Dad kept folded up inside the back cover. I can't figure out what went wrong. Dad didn't mention being sick or tired. He didn't have premonitions about falling. His last journal entry goes like this:

ONE DAY LEFT ON THE MOUNTAIN. DOWN THE MULDROW GLACIER TOMORROW. I CAN'T WAIT TO REACH THE SOFT TUNDRA AND MY SECRET STASH OF PEACHES AND BRANDY AT McGONAGALL. LIFE DOESN'T GET BETTER THAN A DAY ON THIS MOUNTAIN.

Maybe the earthquake rattled some sense into me, because this time I get it. After Dad managed to crawl out of the crevasse on the Muldrow Glacier, he would go to find his secret stash of peaches and brandy to celebrate. He might linger out there for a while — at McGonagall Pass — before coming home.

I could find him out there.

Or, if Dad's really still trapped in the mountain, then every minute matters, and I need to go get him — now.

Finally it's clear what I need to do: go to Denali and hike out to the foot of the mountain. If I find Dad's stash, then I'll know for sure that he's really stuck in the glacier. If not, I'll find Dad himself, eating peaches in the tundra of Denali National Park.

CHAPTER 5

When I wake up in the morning, I slide the broken picture frame under my bed and get started. I need to get ready to go. First I make my bed. Tucking in sheet corners and puffing up the comforter until it's smooth makes me feel better. Then I head for the camping gear in the corner. I stuff my sleeping bag into its compression sack. I pack my personal gear: Long underwear. Fleece jacket and pants. Goose-down parka. Four pairs of wool socks. Winter hat. Gloves. Bandanna. Bug spray. Underwear. Leatherman. Nylon hiking pants. Flower book. Toothbrush. Foam camping pad. Compass. Matches. Binoculars.

When I find the travel Scrabble board, I get dizzy. I'm about to put it in my pile, but I can't, I can't, I can't.

No Scrabble until Dad comes home. It's *our* game — his word game — and I can't play it without him.

Binoculars are the best thing in the pile. They bring everything closer. They will help me spot Dad on the mountain.

I find four stale gummy bears in the side pouch of my backpack. I eat them even though they're hard to chew. Candy is my calm.

When I'm done packing gear, I head downstairs. It's quiet as a spider in the kitchen, and the green bean casserole is still on the counter, stinking up the whole room.

I gather some cooking utensils and try to figure out how in the world I'm going to tell Mom about my plan.

The phone rings and rings. Nobody leaves messages, but on the fourth round of ringing, after the beep, I hear my best friend's voice: "Hi, Lily, it's Jenny. I'm having a blast with my grandma. Hope you're having a great summer so far. Say hi to the family. Talk to you soon."

A part of me wants to grab the phone when I hear her voice, but Jenny doesn't know what's happening, and I'd rather talk to her once I find Dad and he's home. Otherwise, it's too hard to explain.

I rummage through the cupboard under the sink to find my water bottle and cook pot. When I find one of Dad's brandy flasks, it hits me: I need to hurry, hurry, hurry or it's going to be much too late.

Mom walks into the kitchen and sits down at the table with today's crossword puzzle. She's only finished three words. They're easy words too: *grim, cub,* and *road.* It's weird because crosswords are Dad's thing. He's the word guy, not Mom. But Mom's been obsessing over the crossword ever since the call. It's the only thing she has the energy to do, like picking up Dad's words will make a difference.

Every dish she's used is piled on the kitchen counter, and the cereal milk from yesterday is starting to smell, not to mention the gloppy green bean casserole. This is not the normal everything-in-its-place Mom.

I'm not sure how to break my plan to her. I mean, how do I tell Mom that I really need to travel more than two hundred thirty miles north to find Dad?

I hope the biggest kind of hope I can muster and say, "Mom. We need to go to Denali."

She looks up from her crossword puzzle and stares at me like I'm a mosquito about to bite. She picks up her mug of coffee, left over from yesterday, takes a long sip, and gulps.

"No way," she says.

"But I think Dad wants us to go," I say.

"It's not Dad's to decide," Mom says, and I don't like the prickly sadness of her voice.

"Can't we just go for a few days?" I ask.

"No," Mom says. Her voice leaves no room for budge. "I don't want to go back there."

"Ever?" I ask.

"Ever," she confirms, and I swallow my mouthful of gummy bears whole.

But Denali is our place. Mom makes mac and cheese, and Dad studies trail maps. Sophie is even fun. We cook and hike and watch wildlife. At night we line up our sleeping bags side by side like caterpillars inside the tent. Mom and Dad help us fall asleep by counting animals we saw that day: arctic ground squirrels, caribou, snowshoe hares, ptarmigan, moose, grizzly bears, and the rare fox or wolf.

We've gone to Denali every summer since forever —and I'm not about to stop going now, especially when Dad needs us most.

Mom stares at the crossword puzzle so hard I can't believe she's not turning into a word. She must be thinking of all our Denali days too.

"If you won't come along, then can I go on my own?" I ask.

"Of course not," Mom says. "You're only twelve."

"I'll go with Sophie, then," I say. This might be my stroke of genius. Mom's been trying to get Sophie and me to do things together recently, especially outdoor stuff.

"The answer is *no*, Lily."

"But Dad said I could practically climb Denali by myself already. Why can't I go for a piddly little camping trip in the park?"

"You just can't," Mom says, "and that's final."

"Sophie's certified in wilderness first aid," I say, "and you and Dad even let us go camping by ourselves last summer."

"Last summer was different," Mom says.

I can tell I have a lot more work to do, so I head to the counter and pour a cup of yesterday's cold coffee

23

and add chocolate milk, brown sugar, cinnamon, and marshmallows. I pop it in the microwave for a minute. I don't really like coffee, but it makes me feel better to taste something bitter. The day feels more alive. While it's heating, I fill up a bowl with sour apple Nerds. Mom hasn't noticed that I've only eaten candy since Dad went missing. Or if she has noticed, she doesn't care.

With steaming sugary coffee and Nerds in hand, I sit down beside Mom and her crossword at the table.

"What's another word for *daydream?*" she asks, holding her pencil tip to word 3-Across.

I crunch my Nerds slowly. "What's the first letter of the word?" I ask.

"R," Mom says. She knows it because word 3-Down is *road*.

Remember? Recall? Review? No, those aren't right. "How many letters?" I ask.

"Seven."

"*Reverie,*" I say, letting the word slip gracefully off my tongue. It's one of those words that sound even prettier than the meaning. Dad taught me all about reveries when I was studying for the spelling bee last school year.

"R-E-V-E-R-I-E. *Reverie,*" I say.

Mom pencils the word into the puzzle with Dad's special mechanical pencil. She looks funny working on his puzzle, and *reverie* is only the fourth word she's figured out. It will take her all week to finish the puzzle at this rate.

I shove another handful of Nerds in my mouth. I've always been Dad's little crossword helper, but I'm not sure I like being Mom's.

I grab the dictionary to double-check the meaning. *Reverie: A state of abstracted musing; daydreaming.* Yes, that's right.

Reverie. I think that's what I experienced last night after the earthquake. A mountain reverie.

"Mom?" I ask, and she is already on to the next word. "Here's the deal: Sophie and I will go together. We'll ride the train to the park. We know exactly what to do once we're camping. You and Dad always say we know more about camping than any other kids at school." There. I've said it, and Mom knows it's all true.

"You're not going to give up, Lily, are you?"

"Never."

"I can't worry about anyone else," she says. The concern in her eyes is hard to ignore. It's not about-to-cry concern; it's worse. I feel bad for pushing her, but I know how to solve her problem. I will find Dad and make things better.

"I'm not going to be able to live without going to Dad's mountain," I say. "It's that simple."

Mom shakes her head.

"What if we arrange it with the Wonder Lake ranger?" I ask. We know Ranger Collins from our annual camping trips to Wonder Lake. She's always there to welcome us to the campground and tell us about the latest bear sightings and the next sandhill crane migration. She's been our friend there, year after year. "We can tell her that we're coming, and she'll watch out for us." Now I'm onto something, and I can see Mom's face shift. Plus, how hard can it be to outwit a park ranger once we get there?

Mom stares at her puzzle like it will give her answers.

"You know how you're obsessed with these puzzles?" I ask, giving it one last shot.

"Mmm-hmm," Mom says while penciling in *Eden* for *paradise*.

"That's how I feel about Denali," I say. "I need to go there — be there — close to Dad. Pitch a tent on the tundra and hike river bars and see wildlife."

Mom rubs her eyes with her fists and then opens them wide. Wide like she gets it. Then she spins her wedding ring on her left ring finger, as if the spinning can rewind time.

"If you can convince Sophie to go, and Ranger Collins agrees to watch out for you two, then I'll let you go. But only to the campground, and there will be strict rules."

"Sure — anything," I say, and my heart races ahead to the park and the tundra and the mountain . . . and Dad! I'm finally *going*.

CHAPTER 6

"Soph?" I whisper. "Can I come in?" Her shades are drawn, so it's pitch-dark inside.

"Sure," she mumbles.

I leave the door propped open so I have a tiny bit of light. As I walk in, the weight of the mountain sits on my shoulders. I have to convince Sophie of the plan.

Sophie's lying on top of her quilt with her knees up to her chest.

"Will you come with me to Denali?" I say.

Sophie stares at me. "Why?"

"Dad's out there, and you know he's still fighting."

"He's not, Lily. He's somewhere in the glacier. Gone." Sophie's not whispering now, and her voice is crackly like she's about to lose it. "I want him to be alive. I really do. But there's no way." Sophie's eyes fill up with tears, slow tears that can't quite escape her eyelids.

I shove a huge handful of Nerds in my mouth. The tangy apple pebbles remind me that I can't give up.

"There *is* a way!" I say. "Dad could have fallen, and then used all his gear to climb out of the ice and ..."

"They did a full search and found no trace of him," Sophie says, and the reminder feels like darts piercing a balloon. "And he wasn't roped up."

"The earthquake might have shifted the ice," I say.

"You're in la-la Lilyland," Sophie says.

I try to keep my cool. I'm not in la-la *anywhere*, but Sophie is my only way to Denali, so I have to be careful. She slides a charm back and forth on a silver chain around her neck. I've never seen her necklace before; it shimmers in the low light.

"You know what Dad said about the hard times?" I ask after a while.

"I know, I know," Sophie says. "Eat some gummy bears and go for an adventure."

"Darn straight," I say, stealing another one of Dad's lines. "He doesn't want us sitting around here feeling sorry for ourselves."

"True, but look what adventure did for him — made him dead."

Dead. The word sucks the breath out of my lungs. *Dead.* My heart races. I reach for my candy. I put the bowl of Nerds up to my mouth and drink the last bit of them.

Then I say the truest words I can muster: "Dad will know that you love him if you go to Denali."

As the words come out of my mouth, Sophie uncurls from her position on the bed.

"He *will* know," I say, and Sophie sits up taller, still not speaking.

"So pack your bags," I say. "We need to get going."

CHAPTER 7

It's settled. We're departing first thing tomorrow morning for Denali National Park for a four-night trip. I'm still worried that Sophie's going to change her mind. To make matters worse, Mom's going a little batty; she's always been a checklist lady, but this time she even printed out a paper of terms and conditions and made us sign it.

1) No river crossings.
2) No backcountry camping (campground only).
3) No technical climbing.
4) Check in with Ranger Collins upon arrival at Wonder Lake campground.

It's the first two conditions that are the worst,

because we'll definitely have to cross a few rivers and go backcountry camping to get to Dad's mountain. I'm not positive about the third one. We'll have to wait and see, but I'm pretty sure we'll encounter some technical stuff. Ranger Collins shouldn't be a problem; she must have more to worry about than two sisters in the campground.

I steer my eyes away from the paper of terms and conditions when I sign my name. That way it doesn't feel like a big lie. Mom means well, but it's a good thing Dad told me that half the world's rules were meant to be broken.

We talk to Ranger Collins on speakerphone. She agrees to check in with us each night, and Mom thinks we'll be safe as denned grizzly cubs as long as we have a mama bear park ranger watching over us. It's too late to book campground reservations and bus tickets online, so we'll have to buy them when we arrive at the park entrance.

I write a detailed shopping list, and Sophie and I pile into Dad's Ford Ranger pickup and head for Safeway. I'm starting to feel better now that we're really getting ready to go.

When we pull into the grocery store parking lot,

Sophie leaves the truck running like she's not sure she wants to go in.

"Let's divvy up the list," I say. Sophie nods like, *At least we have a list*, or what Dad calls a "plan of attack."

I rip the list in half. I give Sophie the breakfast and lunch items. I'll do dinners and snacks. When I hand Sophie her part, she stares at it for a while and then turns off the ignition.

"Okay, let's go," she says, but she's still buckled into her seat.

I open the passenger door. The parking lot is crammed with cars and bustle. Today is normal for most people. Shopping carts rattle. Friendly families chatter. And the sun shines down like nothing could be wrong in the world.

"Let's meet at checkout in fifteen minutes," Sophie says as we walk through the double doors. Fifteen minutes sounds like forever.

Dinners. We have some freeze-dried meals back home in the cupboard, but I need chili. When I get to the bean aisle, I'm faced with too many choices. Dinty Moore or Stagg Chili? Hot or mild? I just want plain old chili — the good stuff — and all these choices give me the shivers. I pick Stagg because it has the nicest label, and I hope it's the same kind Dad always buys. I can't remember.

When I'm putting the chili cans into my basket, I hear the unmistakable voice of my fifth grade teacher, Mrs. Lee.

"Hello, Lily," she says.

I'm just standing there with my basket, and it's too late to sneak down the aisle and pretend not to know her.

She gives me a hug from behind and says, "I'm so sorry about your dad."

I want her to stop hugging me, so I pretend to cough, but it's not entirely pretend. I can't breathe.

Mrs. Lee finally lets go of me, and I turn to face her. She squints her eyes and shakes her head. Then she gives me a squeeze on my right arm: "Let me know if you ever need anything, sweetie."

I can't move or talk.

"And by the way," Mrs. Lee continues, "many people are wondering when you'll have the service for him. Do you know the date?"

"There won't be a service," I say, and I'm surprised the words are coming, but then they spill out, "because Dad's not dead, he's only missing, and not even my mom thinks he's really gone. That's why I'm going to Denali."

Mrs. Lee raises both eyebrows and says, "Oh my," before grabbing her grocery cart and continuing down the pasta aisle in a sudden hurry.

I can't wait for Dad to come home so that people like Mrs. Lee can say, "Oh my," for a totally different reason.

Onward.

Next stop: the candy aisle.

I toss M&M's into my basket, like the ones we eat while hiking up Bird Ridge every spring. And Toblerone chocolate, from sheep watching on Cathedral Mountain. Snickers, from ice-skating on Westchester Lagoon at Christmastime. And Tootsie Pops — Mom likes red, Sophie and I like brown, and Dad likes the rare purply-pink ones. I reach out to pick our usual colors, but I can't do it. Just looking at them makes my stomach flip. Tootsie Pops bring back Dad, but he's not here, and I can't eat any of them until I find him.

I shove the box of Tootsie Pops so far back on the shelf that they're out of sight. If I can't eat them, I don't want anyone else to either. I'll just have to take some candy from Dad's stash instead.

Done. The heavy basket *thwaps* against my leg as I head to the checkout area. Sophie's waiting for me at aisle three. She looks at my basket first, and then up at my face.

"You look like a stunned caribou," she says.

I *am* one.

I vow I won't go to the grocery store again until Dad comes home.

CHAPTER 8

Before bed, I pack our food into two nylon stuff sacks.

"That's enough for the whole family," says Sophie when she saunters into the kitchen.

"We need extra food for Dad when we find him," I say, and Sophie's eyes widen like she's seen a ghost.

"Every family needs one crazy kid," Sophie says.

The packing is better than the shopping. At least we have a plan in place, which makes me feel so much closer to Dad.

It's almost midnight by the time my backpack is cinched up and my hiking boots are laid out, ready for adventure. I crawl into bed without brushing my teeth or changing into pajamas. Then I imagine all the possible things I could forget. Parka. Got it. Boots. Yes. Pepper spray. Check. Bug spray. Got it. Knife? No.

I can't go camping without a knife!

I hop out of bed and grab my folding knife from the closet. I tuck it into the top flap of my pack. While I'm up and shuffling through the closet, I find my headlamp too. It's light almost all night in June, but what if I need a light during the dusky hours?

I add my headlamp to the pile.

A thought creeps in while I'm lying in bed, willing myself to sleep. What if I find Dad, and he's too injured to walk home?

I need a rescue bag.

I'm up again, tiptoeing down the stairs to the garage — Dad's place.

I find Dad's mountain rescue pack underneath his cluttered workbench, below the candy stash. Inside it is a fold-up shovel, a rope, crampons, heat packs, and a puffy parka. Everything I could need.

While I'm there, I raid Dad's candy stash one last time. I take just a few gummy bears from an already-open bag: three red bears, two green, and one white. They're a little stale, but they'll do.

A horrible thought takes hold of me: What if I can't find him and this is the end of his stash? What if he's never able to shop for candy again?

I push the thought away and carry Dad's rescue bag and my six bears back up to my bedroom. When I get there, I line up the bears on my bedside table.

Three red bears.

"Hey, Dad," I whisper.

Two green bears.

"Hold on a little longer."

One white bear.

"We'll be on our way by morning."

CHAPTER 9

Dad always says, "Ready is a feeling in your belly when you know you can take on the world."

Ready is not how I feel when the alarm clock jolts me out of the nightmare. This time, I'm reaching my hand out to Dad, but our fingers never touch. I can't tell if he's in the glacier or on the tundra, but I reach and reach and reach, and I don't get any closer.

My mouth is sugary dry from didn't-brush-my-teeth-last-night gummy bear breath. I'm still wearing yesterday's dirty blue jeans. I take a thirty-second shower to wash off the nightmare, and then I slip into my nylon hiking pants, my button-down plaid shirt, and a fleece vest. Inside the vest pocket I put Dad's journal and map, one of his Sharpie markers, and my tiny flower book. Finally I tie a red bandanna over my wet hair. I'll braid my hair later when I'm on the train.

I struggle to carry the load down the staircase and out the front door past Mom. It must weigh fifty pounds.

"You're not going to be able to haul all that," Mom says.

"No problem," I say, standing up taller.

Mom shakes her head. "Did you remember your rain gear?" she asks.

"Yes."

"What about your parka?"

"Yes, Mom."

"Matches?"

"Yes."

"Sleeping bag?"

"Stop it. I have everything. Trust me!"

Mom follows me out to the front porch. She's getting hovery and weird again, like she's regretting letting us go.

The porch steps are difficult to maneuver, but the tailgate is down on Dad's truck. I'm tempted to set the pack on the driveway and wait for Sophie to help me hoist it onto the truck bed, but since Mom is watching

— doubting — I'm determined to load it myself. I hurl the beast off my shoulders and into the truck.

There.

"You ready?" I yell up the staircase to Sophie.

"All set," she yells back. She's not smiling as she walks down the steps with a pack half the size of mine.

"That's all you're bringing?" I ask. Did she even bring the basics — a parka and hat and extra socks?

"Yep. This is everything." She's wearing her lime-green high-top sneakers, which are definitely *not* designed for hiking.

"You sure you want to wear *those* shoes?" I ask. What's up with Sophie? She knows what to take camping. But as the words leave my mouth, I realize that I sound just like Mom did a few minutes ago.

"Yes, Mom," Sophie says, confirming my instincts.

My face gets hot and tingly. Good thing I packed extra gear. Sophie doesn't know just how adventurous this trip will be. I probably should have told her about the full plan — to walk to the mountain — but it's late, much too late, to tell her now, with Mom watching and a train to catch. We'll have to make do.

Mom drives us to the train station at Ship Creek in downtown Anchorage and helps us unload our packs onto the platform. Sophie and I have been to Denali dozens of times, but never by train, and never without Mom and Dad.

It's weird at the station, like we're here for a rocket launch to the moon, and all the other people are waiting to go to some other planet. I'm dressed in my camping grubbies, but most of the other people are old — with gray and white hair — and they haul suitcases on wheels like dogs on leashes.

"All set?" Mom asks. Her arms shake — not as much as when she got the call — but they tremble enough for me to notice.

I give Mom a hug, and it's an awkward one. I almost tip over from the weight of everything.

"See you in a few days," I say.

Mom squeezes me tight. "Careful out there," she says. "Check in with Ranger Collins as soon as you arrive."

Under the weight of our packs, Sophie and I teeter up the steps and board the train. When the whistle blows and we pull away from the station, Mom stands on the platform alone. She waves goodbye, a weak and floppy wave. Even though it's cloudy out, she wears sunglasses, the kind with big dark lenses that cover half her face.

It feels like we're leaving a stray animal on the side of the road. All wrong, like we should hop off and call her name and check her collar to see if she has a call-if-found emergency contact number. But Mom is Mom. She's not a stray, and she doesn't want to come this time. What spurs me on is knowing how happy she will be when we bring Dad home.

The train ride lasts forever. Eight hours. The clock is ticking, ticking, ticking, and I'm squirmy in my seat.

Sophie and I go to the food car and get sodas. It helps to pace from car to car, but when my 7Up's gone and I've chewed all the ice cubes and I've braided my hair, there's nothing left to do but worry and wait.

"Why do you think Mom let us go?" I ask Sophie, still hardly believing that Mom agreed to our plan.

"She knows Dad would want us to," Sophie says, and she sounds as sure as her high-top sneakers are green. It's weird how Sophie is so hot and cold and moody. Sometimes she makes no sense, but right now she sounds pretty smart.

Sophie's right. Even though Mom is much more orderly than Dad, she loves his adventurous streak. I think sometimes she wishes she could be more of a free spirit like Dad.

The worst part of the ride happens when the mountain — Denali — comes into view. The rest of the landscape is summery green, but Denali is snow-scoured white, and she's so tall that she's more a part of the sky than the solid earth below.

The other riders on the train gawk at her and say, "Majestic Denali."

She *is* majestic, but I don't want to hear about it from tourists. This is Dad's mountain, and he's up there, and that's scary and beautiful — all mixed together.

All I want right now is to hop on over to the mountain, reach for Dad's hand, take it in mine, and bring him home.

CHAPTER 10

A fat red squirrel sits on the railing in front of the Wilderness Access Center. His whiskers twitch, and he chitters at us when we walk by, as if to say *You're almost there, Lily.* The air smells clean, and the small scraggly spruce trees are my first clue that we've arrived in Denali National Park, a much more northern place.

"Here goes," Sophie says as she swings open the door.

Inside, the line for bus tickets and campground reservations is long, snaking almost out the building. Dozens of tourists shuffle around, pointing at maps and photos on the walls, and making plans to stay at the campgrounds inside the park. I know we have to stay at Wonder Lake, the closest campground to Dad's mountain.

We join the reservations line. Sophie shifts her weight between legs, and I stare down at her lime-green sneakers. It's crazy that she's wearing them. I'm still hoping she stowed away some hiking boots in her backpack, but I know better than to ask.

"Next," says the lady behind the counter. "Are you two *alone*?" she asks.

Sophie nods. I want to tell the lady that *alone* is not the right word for two people together.

"In that case," she says, with raised eyebrows, "how can I help you?"

"We need campground reservations for the next four nights at Wonder Lake," Sophie says.

"All we have for tonight is Savage River Campground," she says.

"Are you *sure*?" I ask, and the word *savage* feels crueler than ever.

"Yes, that's it," she says, looking over us toward the long line of visitors waiting in line.

I prop my elbows up on the counter, mimicking the way Dad always convinced people to bend the rules for him. "Can we pay you double and get out to Wonder by tonight?" I ask.

"No means no," she says, not smiling.

"But Ranger Collins at Wonder is expecting us," I say.

"Doesn't matter," she says. "Full is full."

"It's okay," Sophie says, elbowing me away from the counter. "What's one more day?"

"Could be the difference between dead and alive," I say.

The lady behind the counter squints her eyes.

"We'll take one night at Savage and three at Wonder Lake," Sophie says.

"No," I say, but Sophie puts her hand hard on my shoulder.

"If you hurry, you can get on the four p.m. camper bus to Savage," says the lady, handing Sophie the tickets.

What's the hurry if we can't get to Dad's place?

After Sophie pays, we bolt out of the visitor center.

"I can't believe she wouldn't give us Wonder," I say, kicking a peanut that fell from a tourist's trail mix.

"The whole world doesn't revolve around us," Sophie says, but it should when we have such an important mission.

Before we catch the shuttle, Sophie insists on calling Mom. "We have to tell her that we can't get to Wonder Lake tonight. Otherwise Mom *and* the ranger are going to freak out."

"Fine," I say, but what I think is, *Who cares if they freak out?* Right now, the only thing that matters is that Dad's been missing in the crevasse for four days.

Four days!

How long can he last without food or water? Surely he had at least a granola bar and a water bottle in his backpack.

And I can't push away the nightmare of Dad sliding back into the mountain. It's as if I really saw it happening and I can't escape it.

But I must. I'm the only one on earth who's still on a mission to find him; well, Sophie is too, even though she doesn't know it.

"All set?" I ask, when Sophie returns from the pay phone. There's no cell service in Denali National Park.

"Yes. Mom knows we're headed to Savage, and she's all good."

All good? Nothing is good. And there's that squirrel again. "Chitter, chitter, chitter."

This time, the squirrel's sound makes me uneasy.

CHAPTER 11

It's raining when the bus driver leaves us at Savage River Campground. Weird. It's been a blue-sky day since we left Anchorage, so I'm not sure where the clouds have come from. There's nothing good about getting off the bus into a rain squall, especially when Dad is more than seventy miles farther down the road.

"Are we going to pitch this tent in the rain?" I ask Sophie as we huddle together. I've been here before, and I know there's not a lot of natural shelter at Savage. We're up in the taiga, which Dad always called "the land of little trees." The winters are long and cold here — too long and cold for trees to grow big and tall.

Sophie looks at the sky. "It doesn't seem like the rain will pass anytime soon, so we might as well."

I wonder what it's like for Dad on the mountain in the rain.

I pull up my jacket hood.

Normally we would spend an hour choosing the best spot for camping. Site 13 or site 4? Which one has the nicest view? What about the flattest ground for sleeping? Today Sophie and I don't debate. We run into the first open spot — site 7B — and I drop the tent bag on the ground. This is not our final destination, and any spot will do.

Rain beats down harder, pattering against my jacket. Time to hurry.

The ground is muddy and wet. I dump out the contents of the tent bag and wish I could get the rain to stop long enough for us to turn all these poles and tarps into a tent.

Sophie stands a few feet away, staring at the ground. Why isn't she helping?

"Sophie," I say. She doesn't look up; she doesn't even bother to pull up her hood. She lets the rain pound her.

"Sophie, *please*," I beg. This isn't the Sophie I know.

"I can't do it," she says. "Not without Dad." Her hands are empty, her chin down, and I can tell she means it.

But this is a two-person job.

The rain pummels me. What do I do first? Lay out the tarp? Yes. Then the tent body. Do the tent poles form a triangle or a dome? I can't remember.

I've helped Dad pitch tents dozens of times, but never by myself. It's as if this rain has washed away everything I know about setting up camp.

Water drips down both of my cheeks and slithers down my neck. I need to hurry.

Focus, Lily.

Once I begin linking tent poles, it starts coming back. The poles form a dome and clip into each corner of the tent — as well as its roof. The rain fly goes over everything. Then I pound stakes into the earth to keep the tent from lifting away in the wind.

Of course, the minute I'm finished, the rain slows — now that everything is sopping.

"Thanks for the help," I mutter to Sophie.

Sophie doesn't say anything, and it's her silence that's hard. Sophie's always made a lot of noise, and even if it's not nice noise, at least it reminds me that she's my big sister and this storm will pass. Right now Sophie's silence feels like that pause between lightning striking and thunder rumbling.

My stomach growls.

Lunch. I need to figure out lunch. It's practically dinnertime already.

"You hungry?" I ask.

"I could eat a whole pig," Sophie says, and it's weird that hunger is the one thing that gets her talking.

I wish Mom were here right now to whip up our favorite mac and cheese. And Dad would build a fire, and it would burn even with the wet ground. Not even a flood could snuff out Dad's campfires. Then we'd play a game of Scrabble. We'd sip cups of English breakfast tea with milk and honey while playing, and we'd scheme about where to hike tomorrow.

All this wishing is exhausting, and it feels drenched like my tent and hiking pants.

"What should we eat?" I ask.

"Whatever's fine with me," Sophie says, and that's when I realize that Sophie's not planning to cook, either.

I open our food bag and look for something that I can't mess up. Canned chili. It's hard to ruin canned chili. But it's trickier than I thought to open a can with my Leatherman tool. Sophie watches and chuckles at my efforts until I slam the can on the picnic table. "You do it, then," I say. I grab the stove and try to light it. Dad always made this stuff look easy.

It takes less time than I think it will to heat up the chili, so of course I burn the bottom of the pot. After scarfing down a bowl of burnt chili, I can't sit still. The only way to stop thinking about Dad and the mountain and the crevasse is to *do* something.

"Let's climb up Healy Ridge," I say. Healy Ridge is our family spot, the place we've spent so many summer days in Denali National Park.

"It's kind of late to start that now," Sophie says, eyeing her watch, but I don't think it's just her watch that holds her back.

"The sun shines all night," I say. "We've got plenty of time."

"Humph," Sophie says. She doesn't even argue.

"Well, I'm hiking," I say. "Are you coming or not?"

"I guess so," says Sophie, standing up from the picnic table.

"Get your gear," I say.

"Why do we need *gear*?" Sophie asks.

"Healy is no pip-squeak of a climb," I say, even though she knows it.

A tiny flicker of hope wings its way inside me. I know the chances are slim, but if Dad wandered anywhere, why not up Healy?

Before we head out, I fill my water bottle and grab two bags of gummy bears. I toss them and a winter hat and my Leatherman into my backpack. I clip some bear bells onto the outside of my pack so the jingle will alert the grizzlies. I leave the pepper spray behind. I've never needed to use it, so why would I need it today? This will be a short hike in the park. Nothing to get all fussed up about.

CHAPTER 12

I'm antsy to get hiking, but as soon as we cross the road and we're hiking up the trail, I sense grizzlies everywhere. I feel like a piece of walking bacon. That's what it's like to be at the bottom of the food chain.

My bear bells jingle warning, but bear bells alone won't save us. The jingle jangle on the outside of my backpack offers little comfort right now. We need luck, too, and I wish I had at least brought the pepper spray — just in case.

I know the drill from last time. It's over-the-head willows for the first stretch, and then smooth alpine tundra walking after that. It's the tundra part that I love — the green spongy ground that carpets the earth and makes it soft.

"Hey bear, hey bear!" I say. Grizzlies don't usually bother humans, but today everything feels like it could go wrong. Maybe the lady at the Wilderness Access Center was onto something when she called the two of us "alone."

After yelling "hey bear" twenty-three times, I'm tired of it, so I start our family bear-scare game, even though it makes me feel like a little kid.

"In my grandma's dogsled, I pack an extra-sharp ice ax," I say.

Sophie must be scared of bears too, because first she shakes her head, but then she continues. "In my grandma's dogsled, I pack an extra-sharp ice ax and a chocolate mousse cake."

We go on to pack ten things. I pack what Dad needs: an extra-sharp ice ax, a rope, crampons, a rescue helicopter, and a goose-down parka. Sophie packs what Dad loves: a chocolate mousse cake, a frosty mug of beer, Robert Service poetry, Mom's mac and cheese, and dry socks. I'm about to add the eleventh item when Sophie yells, "Whoa!" Then: "Hey! Whoa!" She claps her hands above her head, and I know this can only mean one thing.

A bear.

The rustling gets louder. Sophie's talking toward the bushes to her right, and I'm waiting for the bear to emerge. I'll drop and play dead, because that's what you do for a grizzly.

"Heads up!" Sophie yells, and the rustling gets louder.

"Hey!" Sophie yells again, and I see it.

A brown beast.

But it's not a bear. It's smaller and prickly.

A porcupine.

He weaves clumsily past Sophie and on through the willows. He comes slowly right for me.

Porcupines don't charge, I tell myself. *They don't eat humans. They're harmless.*

Phew.

At the last second, I step aside to make way for the porcupine. It totters by at a clumsy crawl, and I don't expect it to veer close. But it does.

And it flaps its tail.

Thwap.

"Ouch!" I say, but it's too late. I've got needles pricking, pinching, aching through my right hand.

"Some bear," Sophie says, chuckling, from the willows ahead.

"Help!" I say.

58

"It's just a porcupine," Sophie says. "Calm down." But then she sees my outstretched hand and the quills stuck in it.

"What did you do, pat it?" she asks.

"Not funny," I say, and the prickling gets stronger. "His tail *got* me."

"What now?" Sophie says, grimacing at the sight of the needles.

"I've only seen quills pulled out of dog noses," I say, thinking of when our old dog Snuffy pounced a porcupine a few summers ago.

"Mom used pliers to pluck out those quills," Sophie says.

"Pliers?" I ask. The thought of pliers makes me queasy.

I feel like the stupidest hiker on earth. I know exactly what to do for all the other wild animals. Play dead for a bear. Run from a moose. Throw rocks at a wolf. But a porcupine? I've never heard of humans quilled by porcupines.

Dad never told me what to do for a porcupine. I guess it's obvious — get out of the way. How hard would it have been to step aside?

Sophie's standing like a statue now. "Can you help me or not?" I ask her.

Her face turns white when she looks down at my hand. The quills are tan with dark tips on the ends.

"You know I don't like blood or needles," she says.

"Well, I can't exactly do this myself right now. It feels like I'm getting a flu shot over and over again."

"Okay, okay," Sophie says. "Hold on." She takes off her backpack and rubs her hands together to convince herself she's up to the task. After all, she *is* trained in wilderness first aid.

At least I brought my Leatherman along. To yank. The quills. Out of my hand.

"Sophie. We have to get these out. *Now*," I say, handing over the Leatherman.

She clamps down on the first needle. "One, two, three, go," she says, and she rips the needle out.

"Ouch!" I say.

"Ack!" Sophie yells back, at the sight of blood.

I don't cry. I'm tough. I've got bigger problems than quills.

"Keep going, Sophie," I say. "Keep. On. Going." Once she gets started, I'm desperate to be through with it.

Sophie stops after the third quill. She runs to the tall willows and vomits her chili. Yuck.

"That's going to attract bears," I say.

"Thanks a lot," she says.

Blood continues to pool up from my quill wounds.

"One left," Sophie says, but that last quill is the worst. Sophie yanks back and somehow loses her grip, and the quill is halfway in, halfway out — bent — and jabbing into my skin.

"Get it out," I say. "*Now!*"

It hurts even more when Sophie rips the half-way-out quill from my hand.

Tears start coming and don't stop, and I don't even bother to wipe them away. They are salty tears, not sad tears, and they sting when they drip into my quill wounds. Everything feels like salt in wounds.

"Thanks for your help, Sophie," I say, meaning it. I wrap my bandanna around my hand, and we continue.

CHAPTER 13

Blisters form on the outer sides of my big toes as we hike up Healy, and my quill wounds throb. I'm sure Sophie's getting blisters too, especially because of the green high-tops, but she'll never admit it. She's walking faster now, like somehow the porcupine incident brought her back to her old self.

The bushwhacking ends, and we pop out into the wide green carpet of earth. That's when I smell it for the first time this trip. Wet tundra. Lichens and blueberry bushes and damp spongy ground. If I could bottle up the tundra and turn it into perfume, I would. It's not sweet like roses. Tundra is earthy and gritty, the smell of adventure — and the smell of Dad.

There are dozens of wildflowers, too. I can't identify all of them, but I definitely know some. Dark white windflower. Yellow frigid arnica. Pale blue weasel-snout. White Labrador tea. And my favorite of all, the cream-colored alplily.

It's always hard to believe that these flowers pop up every spring after winters with temperatures as cold as negative fifty degrees Fahrenheit. But if these flowers can survive winter, surely Dad can last more than four days out here now.

After a while, Sophie stops for a bathroom break. When she heads off for the perfect divot in the tundra to squat, I reach into my vest pocket for my tiny flower book.

When Dad gave me the flower book for my fourth birthday, he attached a magnifying glass to it on a pink ribbon. On the first page of the book, he wrote:

HAPPY 4TH BIRTHDAY TO MY ALPLILY.
HERE'S TO HELP YOU SEE THE DELIGHTS OF THE TUNDRA.
THE MAGNIFYING GLASS IS YOUR TICKET TO TINY.
LOVE, DAD

When I was four, I was in love with tiny. I liked runts, dwarfs, mice, ladybugs, dollhouses, miniature books, and fun-size candy bars. I liked tiny in the wilderness, too: dryas, blueberries, spiders, pebbles, shrews, and chickadees. I liked watching squirrels stash mushrooms in treetops more than gaping at a gangly old moose. I liked the way small streams trickled, quieter than wide rivers. Mom always said that when I got bigger, I would be less obsessed with tiny, but she was wrong. I like tiny too much.

Tiny flowers, especially, like forget-me-nots. Forget-me-nots were tiny enough to sit on the kitchen table in my dollhouse. And I sat in patches of them when I climbed Healy Ridge with Dad a few years ago.

We didn't see sheep that day. No bears, either. Not even a hoary marmot. But there were forget-me-nots *everywhere*. It was like a raven had spread a million seeds over the mountain. We weren't supposed to pick flowers in a national park, but Dad winked and let me press a clump of them inside my book.

When I flip through the weathered pages of the flower book now, I get to the blue flower section and find the tiny pressed forget-me-nots. I set the magnifying glass over them, and more details come back.

I see Dad walking up Healy. He limps slightly, since his right leg is longer than his left. Tufts of long brown hair stick out from his ball cap. I see us sitting in a huge patch of forget-me-nots while we eat gummy bears. I see the peak above, and the Savage River below.

Tiny brings back Dad.

"All set?" Sophie asks, and I close my book and stuff it back in my vest pocket. We start walking, walking, walking again, but I can't get forget-me-nots and tiny things and Dad out of my mind.

When we're nearing the summit, I spot a man ahead, walking his final steps to the tippy top.

Plaid shirt. Tan pants. A slight limp.

"Dad!" I holler.

"Wait!" Sophie says.

But I know it's him.

"Dad!"

I scramble up the rocky slope.

He's there. Dad's up there.

So close.

"Dad," I say again. I can't believe this is happening.

When I finally hurl myself up to the top, I yell one last time. "Dad!"

He turns around.

I run toward him, arms outstretched for the hug.

But this man is not Dad.

"Hello?" the man says, a question more than a greeting, and he squints as if to be sure that I'm a real person. "Having a nice hike, young lady?"

I shake my head up and down, but it's only out of habit. The man takes one last look, turns, and keeps on hiking over the back side.

I collapse onto the scree.

The bright blue sky arcs above me, and everything is wrong, wrong, wrong.

"Are you crazy?" Sophie asks when she reaches me.

"I really thought it was him," I say.

"Lily, you can't chase hikers hoping that they're Dad."

Sophie's right, but she doesn't know how real he was to me. The shirt. The pants. The limp. The spirit.

Why couldn't that man have been Dad?

CHAPTER 14

It's late when we finally get back to the Savage River Campground. Sophie and I eat king-size Snickers bars for dinner, and then we crawl into the tent.

It's nice at first, being so close to the earth. No pavement. No floor. No bed. Lying here, I almost feel the pulse of the land, like I'm in the earth's rocking chair.

But once I'm in the tent, I start thinking, thinking, thinking. About Dad and the mountain and how long it will be until I get to them both. I wriggle my way into my sleeping bag, but it doesn't feel caterpillar cozy like usual. The tent is damp, and there's a tree root underneath my sleeping spot in just the wrong place so I can't get comfortable.

Sophie's sitting up in her sleeping bag. She's holding the silver chain and moving the charm back and forth along it. She must also feel how weird it is to have two of us in the tent — not four.

"What's with the necklace?" I ask.

"Oh, just a chain," she says, and quickly tucks it beneath her wool shirt.

"No, it's not. Let me see it," I say, reaching out.

Sophie shakes her head.

"Is it something fancy from Clint?"

"No. Not from Clint," she says, pulling the chain out from her shirt. "Dad gave it to me for my birthday."

My hand aches from the quill wounds, so I shake it and open my fingers and then ball them back into a fist. Open, close. Open, close.

"It's a silver feather," Sophie says. Sophie's birthday was in January, and I don't remember the gift. It must not have seemed important at the time.

Sophie grips the feather between her thumb and index finger so I still can't see it.

"I hated this feather when he gave it to me," Sophie continues. "I wanted the necklace to be from Clint. And I didn't want a feather. I wanted something with more sparkle."

Sophie stops talking and lies back like she wants to disappear into her mummy sleeping bag.

"Is that what's up with the sneakers, too?" I ask.

Sophie nods. "I don't even like the green sneakers, but Dad was so excited when he gave them to me. He thought they were hip." It's true. Dad always tries to do things to make Sophie happy.

"I don't think Dad wanted you to wear them camping," I say.

"You're not kidding," Sophie says. She opens her palm and lays the charm on top of her wool shirt in full view.

The feather is small and shimmery.

"It's beautiful," I say, and it is. In that moment — looking down at the silver feather necklace — I wish that I had my own silver feather from Dad. A shiny little emblem of hope.

It's only ten minutes later and Sophie's asleep, burrowed deep in her sleeping bag so that the silver feather and her face are totally covered up.

In the silence of the tent, I can almost hear Dad whisper his favorite poem by Robert Service. He always reads it aloud on Denali camping nights, a little section from "The Call of the Wild."

Let us probe the silent places,
    let us seek what luck betides us;
      Let us journey to a lonely land I know.
There's a whisper on the night-wind,
    there's a star agleam to guide us,
      And the Wild is calling, calling . . . let us go.

I open up Dad's map, the one folded in the back of his journal. I smooth it out on top of my sleeping bag, and that's when I see them — stars at different landmarks near the mountain. The stars must be all of Dad's important stops on his climb.

A lump forms in my throat, like I swallowed an ice cube whole. These are stars to guide us. I've heard the names of many of the places before: McKinley River. Turtle Hill. Clearwater Creek. Muldrow Glacier. McGonagall Pass. The Great Icefall. Karstens Ridge. These are the main stops on Dad's trip. These are all the same places that Dad wrote about in his journal.

I'm ready to know these stars for myself. On the map, it looks like we'll have a twenty-mile hike to McGonagall Pass and the Muldrow Glacier. I know we'll have rivers to cross, tundra to hop, and animals to encounter.

There are a few stars with dark circles around them. They are not camping spots, because who camps in the McKinley River or Clearwater Creek?

These circled stars must be warning stars. Danger stars.

Maybe they'll keep us from making mistakes?

Good thing I'm better in the wilderness than I am in a school classroom. I'm a survivor. Just like Dad. All we need to do now is get to Wonder Lake and set out for McGonagall Pass and the glacier tomorrow. When we get to McGonagall, we'll find Dad and bring him home.

Simple as sunrise.

His tiny stars will guide us along the way.

CHAPTER 15

The next day, we board the bus at eight a.m. after eating a not-so-delicious gloppy oatmeal breakfast. The bus smells of sweaty feet and rotten apples. I want to hop off as soon as I get on. But I don't, because we're finally on our way to Dad.

The bus driver stops for views along the way. There are Dall sheep on the rocky part of Cathedral Mountain that look like white dots from so far away, and a group of seven caribou cross the road near the Toklat River. Normally I love watching the animals and searching with binoculars to find grizzly bears camouflaged in the tundra, but today all I feel is the tick, tick, tick of the clock. I don't want to stop for anything until we find Dad.

Then I'll be ready for wildlife watching again.

I'm twitchy from all the sitting and waiting, so I eat gummy bears until I slip into a sugary sleep.

I wake up when my head bonks the seat in front of me.

"We're here," Sophie says. Here. Wonder Lake Campground.

I shake my head to get rid of the groggy. My watch says two p.m., and I can't believe I slept through so much of the drive. I have a horrible gummy taste in my mouth.

Getting off the bus sounds like a lot of work, and I still haven't told Sophie about our big trek to find Dad.

The sign makes it official: WONDER LAKE CAMP-GROUND. MILE 85. DENALI NATIONAL PARK. When we step out of the bus, the sun is out of sight. Clouds hang low like fog, hiding the mountain. I slip my hand into my vest pocket to make sure I still have Dad's journal and map, and my flower book. Yes.

"Ready?" Sophie asks, looking down the dirt road toward the campground. But just a glimpse at the road takes away my readiness. This road leads to our family spot. I think of beautiful autumn nights with Mom and Dad and a different Sophie. Blueberry picking. Mountain gazing. Ranger talks. Reading poetry in sleeping bags at night.

It's not the same road today.

I buckle my pack straps, groan, and put one boot forward. Then another.

"Let's do this," I say, trying to feel ready.

At least it's not raining. But there are mosquitoes everywhere!

Zzz. Thwap. Zzz. Thwap.

I'm not sure what's worse — the reality that we're here just the two of us, or the constant buzz and bite of these skeeters.

We're almost to the campground when I spot Ranger Collins and her wide-brimmed hat.

"Welcome back to Wonder Lake, Lily and Sophie," she says. She looks nervous as she walks closer, like she's afraid of talking to two girls who are on a trip to remember their father. Little does she know why we're really here.

"Good to see you again," Sophie says, and she reaches out her right hand to shake a proper greeting.

Even though we've seen Ranger Collins every summer, she feels like a stranger today, not a friend.

"Hi." That's all I can manage. I keep on swatting the mosquitoes, and it feels like they're biting me inside and out.

"There are lots of good tent sites open," says Ranger Collins, "and tonight we have a new ranger giving the talk."

"Thank you," I mumble.

"Let me know if you need anything while you're here, and I'll stop by the campground this evening to check in."

"Thank you so much," Sophie says in her adult voice, and I just nod. How can Sophie pretend that life is normal right now? When she's not being dramatic, sometimes she can be so cool and calm, like a paper doll that talks.

"You need help with your packs?" Ranger Collins asks, eyeing me all hunched over.

"Nope. I'm all set," I say, and I stand up taller.

"Have a nice afternoon, then," she says, and Sophie and I make our way to the campsites.

Sophie hunts for a perfect camping spot while I fill up water bottles for dinner and stash our food in the bear locker. I'm surprised that Sophie wants to help pitch the tent this time. Maybe she feels how close we are to Dad. Or maybe she's moving into her summer ptarmigan feathers.

It might have only been spring when Dad left for the mountain, but it's full summer when the mosquitoes are out like this. A swarm of them follows me. *Zzz.* In my ear. *Zzz.* On my neck. Through my bandanna. "Ouch!" I say, and Sophie swats at them too. Sophie squirts bug spray on me, but it doesn't help. The mosquitoes zig and zag. They buzz and swarm. And it's not exactly clear where they're going, but they're biting, biting, biting.

One hour and forty-three dead mosquitoes later, Sophie and I carry our Top Ramen early dinner down to Wonder Lake. We have to walk while we eat, or the mosquitoes will feast on us.

"You glad to be here?" I ask, trying to make small talk until I figure out how to tell Sophie about the plan.

"Sure," she says, "except for the bugs." *Whap!* She kills two of them on her right hand. "But I hope the mountain comes out for us tomorrow," she says.

We both know that when the mountain comes out, she's huge and beautiful here at Wonder Lake.

"The mountain needs to do a lot more than 'come out' for us," I say.

"What?" Sophie asks, and I know that I need to tell her.

I need to tell her *now*.

"Sophie, there's this adventure I have in mind," I say. I slurp ramen noodles quickly, burning my tongue but not caring. "I think we need to hike out to the mountain."

Sophie stops in her sneakers, not caring about the mosquitoes that hover immediately in her face.

"Please tell me you're kidding," she says, eyes wide. A mosquito lands on her forehead and she doesn't bother swatting it away.

"Nope," I say. "Serious."

I motion Sophie to keep moving to the bench next to Wonder Lake. There will be fewer mosquitoes by the lake because of the breeze.

"It'll take days to get to the mountain," Sophie says.

"No way. It's only twenty miles or so."

"Twenty miles of danger," she says, sitting down on the bench. "And we promised Mom we'd stay at the campground."

"But I have Dad's expert map," I say, "so we can follow his route."

"Follow his route to where?" Sophie asks. "To find his grave?"

Her words are icy. It's hard to shake off that word — *grave*. It's as bad as *dead* to me.

Sophie's quiet as stone, and I'm convinced she's about to say no, that she's not going anywhere. Instead she shakes her head and asks, "What exactly are you planning to do when you get there?"

"I'll either find Dad, or I'll find his stash of peaches and brandy," I say.

"What stash?" Sophie asks.

I pull the journal from my pocket. Sophie needs to read it for herself if she's going to agree to the trip. I hand her the journal, and it feels like I'm asking my fairy godmother to grant me one wish.

One big mountain of a wish.

The bench we're sitting on is wet, and it soaks through the butt of my pants. Sophie flips through the pages, smiling at the good parts, like the line that says,

I miss my girls. Wish they could have seen the view from the summit. When Sophie gets to the end, there are two mosquitoes on her left cheek. She must feel them, but she lets them bite.

"Lily?" she asks.

"Yes."

"You really think Dad's alive?"

"I do," I say.

"I'm not going to hope that hard," Sophie says, "but I think Dad might want us to finish the trip for him, since he couldn't finish it for himself, you know."

"So you'll do it? Come out to McGonagall Pass to the foot of the mountain?" I ask.

"Let me see the map again," she says. I hand it over, and she traces the route with her pointer finger. Down the McKinley Bar Trail, across the river, up Turtle Hill, and out to McGonagall Pass. "Yes, I've heard of all of these places from Dad," she says. Seeing Sophie trace Dad's route from star to star makes everything feel real and possible and exciting.

That's when we hear the trumpeting.

Two white birds swoop down and make a *splooosh* when they land on Wonder Lake and skid clumsily to a halt. Trumpeter swans. They reach their necks up tall toward the sky, and then together they slip their long necks beneath the surface of the lake, tail feathers lifted to the sky.

"You know that they mate for life?" Sophie asks, eyeing the swans.

"Hmm," I say, because I didn't know that, but I wish that I had.

"It's not like high school, where people hop from one to another," Sophie says.

"Is Clint your swan?" I ask, and I can't believe I'm asking it. We never talk about Clint.

"Of course not," Sophie says. She flicks away a few mosquitoes.

"Why not?"

"He's just, well, Clint's just so good-looking," Sophie says, grinning.

"Oh," I say, not sure how good-looking can be worth all that trouble.

"Do you think Mom and Dad were trumpeter swans?" Sophie asks.

"I don't know," I say, but I don't like the way she's talking about Mom and Dad in the past tense.

"I think they were," Sophie says, holding the feather charm between her right thumb and index finger.

"You do?"

"Yes." I haven't heard Sophie so sure about anything in a while. She's being the older sister right now. The one I always used to go to for help.

"But then why was Mom upset with him before he left?" I ask.

"She was worried she'd lose him to the mountain," Sophie says.

"We can fix that," I say. "We can bring her swan home."

"Lily, there are some things you can't change, no matter how hard you try." Sophie sips the last ramen broth from her mug. She sounds a lot like Mom, all practical and sensible.

I shake my head, not taking that for an answer. "So?" I ask, when I can't stand the silence anymore.

"So what?" Sophie says, but she knows what I'm asking.

"Will you come with me to Dad's mountain?"

"You're crazy, Lily," she says, "but I'll go."

I'll go. These are the words of my wish granted. The words of Sophie chasing adventure. She might not think Dad's out there anymore, but her willingness to come with me is all I need. It's enough.

"Ranger talk in ten minutes," a man yells from the dirt path above the lake. This must be the new guy that Ranger Collins told us about.

"Thanks," I yell back. "You want to go?" I ask Sophie.

"No. I'm ready for a nap," she says.

"Nap?"

"Yes. I need to curl up and sleep for a while." Sophie's rapidly slipping into hibernation mode.

"We need to leave for the mountain tonight," I say. Now that Sophie's agreed to go, I'm antsy to set off as quickly as possible.

"Where will we camp?" Sophie asks.

"We're going to have to move fast and just nap when the sun goes down."

"Very funny," Sophie says. She knows that the sun never really goes down at this time of year. "You aren't planning to let us sleep?"

"We won't have time," I say. "Mom expects us back in three days — or else."

Sophie raises her right eyebrow.

"Don't worry, Sophie. I'll pack a lot of food," I promise. "Scout's honor."

"I need to sleep for at least three hours before we start out," Sophie says. "Plus, we can't leave when all the other campers are watching us. They'll be suspicious.

And Ranger Collins will catch us before we even set foot on the trail if we're carrying all our gear."

Sophie's right that we'll need to sneak out, but I don't want to wait until tomorrow.

"Soph, you take a nap while I go to the talk. I'll join you in the tent in a little while. We'll leave for the mountain late tonight after everyone has gone to bed."

What's a few more hours?

"Hold on a little longer, Dad," I whisper, as I make my way to the ranger talk.

CHAPTER 16

I love ranger talks. At least, I used to love them. After Mom's famous camping dinners, the four of us always went together. It didn't matter if the topic was bears or park history or animal tracks. We went, and we always sat together on one long log bench.

Dad went for inspiration. Mom went for information. Sophie for people watching. And I just loved all of it: the gathering, sitting, and sharing stories.

When I arrive at the outdoor amphitheater, there are a few other people, each in couples or family arrangements. I didn't realize what *together* meant until just now, walking up to the ranger talk alone.

I'm tempted to turn around and leave, but I have a few hours to kill, and there's no way I'll be able to nap at a time like this!

I sit down on a bench all alone.

"Good evening," says the ranger who's not Ranger Collins. He wears a tan brimmed hat and smiles a Smokey Bear smile. "I'll wait one more minute in case others are joining us." He looks over to me on my empty bench.

I turn around, pretending to look for my family. I know they're not coming, but I hope the ranger doesn't know. Maybe he'll forget I'm by myself once he starts talking.

"Welcome to Wonder Lake," he says. "Tonight I'm going to talk about the mountain."

The mountain is so big in my mind that it's hard to listen to someone else talk about her. Do these tourists even know what mountain he is referring to?

The ranger points behind him. "If the mountain were out tonight, that's where it would be." Why does he call the mountain *it*? I'm positive that Denali is a she.

Then he asks, "Can anybody tell me how tall the mountain is?"

I raise my hand, instinctively. That's what I do when I know an answer.

He points to me, the only raised hand in the group.

"Twenty-thousand three hundred and ten feet," I

say. That's nothing. Every Alaska girl knows that, or she should.

"You're smart," he says, but I don't feel smart when he asks the next question. "What is your name?"

"Lily," I say, and I immediately wish I hadn't said it. No more anonymous.

The ranger stares at me for a long — too long — moment, and then he turns and says, "Thank you, Lily." I can tell by his look that he knows. He knows, or thinks he knows, that I'm the missing climber's Lily.

My right eye twitches. Why did I open my big mouth?

I settle onto the bench, but I'm not even a little bit calm. I pull out my gummy bears.

Green bear.

"The first man to summit the mountain was Walter Harper," he says, but I don't imagine Walter. I imagine Dad with his frosty bearded grin.

Yellow bear.

The ranger's voice is smooth and easy to listen to, but I don't really hear him. Instead I'm thinking about those trumpeter swans, and the miracle of Sophie agreeing to go out to the mountain. Even if she's going for different reasons than I am, it's still huge.

White bear.

"During a typical summer," the ranger says, "there are casualties on the mountain." His words interrupt like a punch. *Casualty?* What kind of word is that? It sounds more like a crossword-puzzle word than a word that means the same thing as *dead*.

Red bear.

"Common hazards are frostbite, hypothermia, falling, and crevasses . . ."

Crevasse is the only word I hear now. It's another word that's better in a crossword than in real life. Ice hole. Gaping ice trench. Trap.

Two red bears.

"The summit is the tallest point in North America."

Three green bears.

"The mountain is thought to be a sacred place."

Five yellow bears.

I'm shaking all over, swatting at mosquitoes, and my eyes continue to twitch, twitch, twitch. All this mountain talk makes me jumpy, like the mosquitoes are swarming my insides.

At the end the ranger asks, "Does anybody know someone who has climbed the mountain?"

My hand shoots up. Dad. My dad climbed the

mountain many times. The other campers stare at me from their benches, and I wish again that I hadn't raised my hand.

The ranger looks at me, and I think he is about to ask me who, and I don't want to answer. Instead he smiles and says, "That is an incredible feat," and the way he says it makes me sure that he knows — that I'm the missing climber's kid.

Why have you given up on him too? I almost ask, but I keep those words inside me, swarming.

I can't sit still anymore.

I stand and run up the dirt path away from the amphitheater. I race past the bear locker and beyond the outhouses and tent sites. A few wide-eyed campers flit apart, somehow knowing to get out of my way.

I keep at a full gallop until I get to our berry patch. Ours. Dad's and mine. It's above everything, secluded. I leap from the road into the squishy tundra. Then I bend over and breathe in deep. Wet tundra and lichens.

No blueberries. It's too early for ripe berries.

I lie down on the tundra with bugs buzzing and my head spinning. I put my face into a blueberry bush, just to see if I can bring back the smell. Nope.

Dad calls blueberries a religion of their own. "Here's

another chapel of the holy blueberry," he says every time he finds a good patch.

Sitting in the berryless tundra brings back the day, years ago, when Dad and I ate ourselves sick with berries.

Sophie and Mom had wanted to go on a "real hike" that day, and I was spitting mad that that they wouldn't let me come. I could keep up with them just fine.

"Lily, let them go," Dad said. "We'll have more fun without them."

And we did.

Dad and I sat in the berry patch and filled four water bottles.

I can't remember the exact stories Dad told, but I remember him reciting part of that Robert Service poem again.

> Let us probe the silent places,
>> let us seek what luck betides us;
>> Let us journey to a lonely land I know.

I didn't always remember the first line, but I'd chime in for the second: *Let us journey to a lonely land I know.* I also remember that Dad didn't bother to pick the berry leaves out of each handful.

"Don't we need to get the leaves out?" I asked him.

"Life is too short to pick the leaves out of the berries," he said. "Grizzlies don't pick out the leaves, so neither do we."

I remember Dad's blueberry grin and the way he believed, with complete certainty, that life was too short for dawdling around.

No more dawdling for me either.

I sit up in the tundra and brush off the mossy green and twiggy branches.

It's time to get packing. Sophie might want to sleep, but I need to get ready.

CHAPTER 17

When I get back, Sophie's sitting at the picnic table in front of our tent. The cookstove hums with a bright flame, and Sophie sits across the table from that familiar tan wide-brimmed hat.

Ranger Collins.

I really don't want to talk to her. I'm afraid she'll figure out our plan and she'll stop us. So I'm standing at the end of the tundra path, staring, trying to decide where I can run this time, when Sophie settles the matter. "Lily. Come over here," she says, and just like that, I'm stuck. I can't run now.

I walk slowly toward them.

"I need some sleep," I say rudely when I reach the table, hoping the ranger will take her cue to leave.

"Hold on," Sophie says. "Did you know that Ranger Collins saw Dad?"

I can hardly keep my feet on the path. I nod. All I know is that she thinks Dad's dead.

"It's good to see you both," the ranger says. "Charley's girls."

Her words are like a punch. I wish I could feel like one of Charley's girls now, instead of a girl held hostage by a park ranger.

"What are you planning to do while you're here?" Ranger Collins asks, a quick change of subject.

Gulp. "Oh. We're going to take some long, long hikes," I say. I glare at Sophie to remind her not to spoil our plan.

"Yes, long hikes and just hang out with the mosquitoes. That's about it," Sophie says. Sophie's good at grown-up lying. She sounds calm, like a trouble-free adult.

Not like me.

Franticness wells up inside me. Twitching eyes. Gurgling belly. Shivering that won't stop. Swatting at mosquitoes.

"I'm hiking out to the McKinley River Bar tomorrow," Ranger Collins says. "Do you two want to come? There are good views of the mountain from there."

Sophie's about to answer, but I interrupt her.

"Umm. No," I say. "I think we'll just keep to ourselves."

Ranger Collins looks to Sophie for a second opinion.

"Yes, I think we'll stay put," Sophie says. "It's been a long week." That's the ultimate understatement. "But if we get a burst of energy, maybe we'll see you out there."

I'm relieved that Sophie's playing it cool cat. She doesn't want to ruin our secret either. But I'm *not* relieved that the ranger is going out to the river tomorrow too — on the same path we're planning to take to get to the mountain.

We need to get going soon so we don't meet her on the trail.

"What time are you hiking?" I ask, trying to make it sound like no big deal. "Just in case we change our minds."

"Around seven a.m., in the cool of the day before the mosquitoes come out in full force," she says.

About seven. That could mean before seven or after seven, and there's no way to tell.

A rush wells up inside me now. Sophie and I need to get a move on. Right away. We can't be running into the ranger out there. She'll stop our mission for sure.

Sophie changes the subject, which seems good at first.

"So, tell me when exactly you saw Dad on the expedition?" she asks.

"I saw him when he was on his way to the mountain," she says, "and then I was also part of the team that —"

"So you gave up on him?" I interrupt.

The ranger takes off her hat, eyes wide. She doesn't respond at first, like she's frozen in shock.

"I'll leave you two to some peace," she says, after an awkward silence. "Enjoy your time, and let me know if you girls need anything . . . *anything.*" Her words might be nice, but all I hear in them is her belief that Dad's forever gone.

"You look like you've seen a ghost," Sophie says, once the ranger has left. "What's up?"

"I just can't deal with her," I say. "She's like everyone else who has stopped believing."

"You can't blame her for that," Sophie says.

"Well, I do."

Sophie shakes her head.

"We need to depart by ten," I say. "This is your last chance for a catnap."

"Can't we just start early in the morning, before seven a.m.?" Sophie asks.

"No," I say. "Too risky. It's now or never."

CHAPTER 18

Two hours later, the campground is eerie, the air thick with fog and drizzle. It's so cold that my breath creates its own cloud. Not the best weather to start our adventure, but it's dismal enough to scare the other campers into their tents for the night.

A raven feather sits on the trail leading to the outhouse. It wasn't there when Sophie and I went inside the tent, so the bird must have circled us during our catnap. I slip the feather into my pocket for good luck. It's not shiny like Sophie's silver necklace, but it's from a real bird, which gives it an extra chance of a lucky kick.

It's a little scary to be the only person up and walking around the campground, but it reminds me of one of Dad's favorite sayings: "Sleep is for weaklings."

I am not a weakling!

Dad told me that his best ideas come to him from mountaintops. Mom said that her best ideas come to her in the shower. And Sophie said, though she made me promise not to tell, that her best ideas come after kissing boys. Yuck. I don't want to think about Sophie kissing boys.

For me, outhouses do the trick. They're simple. No mirrors. No lights. All I need is a little outhouse on a piece of tundra for good ideas.

When I reach the outhouse door, I knock.

No answer. I pull open the creaky door and step inside.

It's clean, but cold. *Really* cold. The seat feels like a ring of ice. Eek!

When I'm done with my business, a wave of hurry passes over me. Tonight's finally the night.

A part of me wishes this outhouse were a hot air balloon and it could lift me up off the tundra to float into the sky. Up. Up. Up. From above, I could see everything from the raven's-eye view. I could float over to the base of the mountain and find Dad. I could even float up to Denali's summit and catch the view from the top.

When I find Dad, he could join me in my floating outhouse, and we could hover back to the campground and surprise Sophie.

Sophie could tell Dad that she loves him . . . and we could bring him home to Mom.

Feet patter on the trail outside the outhouse, interrupting me. I'm not the only one awake.

The pattering doesn't exactly sound like human feet. "Hello," I say.

No answer. Spooky.

I peek out. A red fox trots down the path toward me. Blood drips from his jowls, and that's when I see it. A freshly dead ground squirrel chomped in his teeth.

My stomach somersaults and I almost vomit. It's not the blood. It's not even the limp squirrel. It's the reality that death happens so quickly around here. I can't help but wonder if Dad is like that little squirrel, chomped in the jaws of the Muldrow Glacier.

No, Lily. Don't give up hope.

I shake the thought away.

I take a deep breath. Dad's a fighter. He's predator, not prey.

When I step out of the outhouse, the rush to get to the mountain is in me. Like a bear knows when to crawl into her winter den to hibernate. Like a crane knows when to migrate. Like a tree knows when to drop her leaves. I know it's time to go.

No more dawdling around.

CHAPTER 19

A ll set?" I ask Sophie. Our bags are finally packed, leaning against the inside shelves of the bear locker. I've packed plenty of food for a three-night trip — and I even brought enough food for Dad when we find him.

Sophie still looks half-asleep, but she's up. Although it's ten p.m., there's plenty of light in the gray sky.

"One quick trip to the outhouse," she says, "and then I'll be ready."

Sophie walks down the trail toward the outhouse, and that's when I notice the graffiti on the walls of the bear locker. All sorts of messages scribbled inside. *Mary loves Joe. Denali Rocks. Wish you were here, Ted. I love Willie. M+R=love.* It's crazy to think about all the stories etched into the wood. I wish Dad had left a message saying *I love Lily.*

I pull out the Sharpie from my vest pocket. I know I'm not supposed to write on walls, but everyone else has, and I can't stop myself.

I need to get the words down to make them real.

See you soon, Dad. Love, Lily

Sophie returns just as I snap the lid back onto the pen and stuff it into my vest pocket.

"Ready?" she asks, eyeing the message but not mentioning it.

"Yes."

We hoist our packs onto our backs.

Ready at last.

Next stop — McGonagall Pass, the footstool of Dad's mountain.

Dad doesn't like the word *rain*. He calls it *cloud water*. Cloud water smacks our raincoats when we get to the trailhead. I'm grateful for some rain, because it keeps the mosquitoes away, but then again, too much rain can get miserable in a hurry.

Stay calm, Lily.

At the trailhead, a hand-carved wood sign says

MCKINLEY RIVER BAR. 3 MILES. There's no sign that says DENALI. APPROX. 20 MILES.

Sophie motions for me to go first. "This was your idea," she says.

Wildflowers line the trail for the first mile of gently rolling tundra. The purple flowers catch my eye. Monkshood and Jacob's-ladder. Dad taught me that monkshood is poisonous, as if the name monkshood weren't eerie enough. And Jacob's-ladder used to make me think of the Bible story in which Jacob dreams of a ladder to heaven. Tonight I hope that these purple flowers will lead me to Dad, not heaven.

We have been walking about a mile when I see the tracks. Fresh, with prints just starting to fill up with cloud water.

One paw, five pads, and five claws. Grizzly bear, for sure.

I'm all of a sudden really glad I brought the pepper spray. We might need more than bear bells for this long journey.

"What are you looking at?" Sophie asks.

I point.

"That's no porcupine," she says.

Following a grizzly is no good. Turn around—that's what anybody with a brain would do. But if we turn around, then what? The clock is ticking, and this is our one chance. Ranger Collins will be here in a few short hours, and we need to be far ahead of her.

"Hey bear, hey bear!" I holler, and continue down the trail.

"Hey bear! Hi bear!" Sophie yells behind me. She doesn't tell me to turn around.

Squish. Squish. Squish. I set my boots hard into the mud, covering up the bear tracks as I go.

It's a relief when the trail opens up into a swampy meadow. Wooden boardwalks run through the center of the meadow, and there's better visibility. No bear in sight. There are some new patches of blue sky above, so maybe the fog and drizzle are lifting.

I turn back to make sure Sophie is still there, and my right boot slips on the slimy boardwalk. *Wham!* I hit the wood hard.

"You okay?" Sophie asks.

"Fine," I say, lying on my side, and I *am* totally fine. But nothing about chasing bear tracks through the mud in the middle of the night to find Dad feels fine or okay.

"If we're going to go, Lily, then we need to get going," Sophie says. Fair enough. Sophie doesn't want to linger too long with the bears, and I can't blame her.

The trail quickly enters a black spruce forest. It's narrow, and the grizzly tracks are still fresh in front of us. I've walked down this trail before without a single worry in my world — Mom and Dad leading the charge. But tonight everything rustles in a spooky Halloween kind of way.

Squirrels? Birds? Bears? I'm hoping for porcupines this time, because I know the trick — get out of the way.

Along with the rustling, the rush of the McKinley River gets louder. I've been to the river many times before, but not in the middle of the night. And I never noticed how loud the river rush could be.

Sophie's leading now, and she's walking so fast that I pretty much have to gallop to keep up. She's on a mission. I can't tell if she's in a hurry to get to Dad, or just to get out of the grizzly forest. We don't play In My Grandma's Dogsled today. It's all business.

"Hey bear, hey bear!" we say, over and over and over again.

After nearly three miles of walking, when our voices are hoarse from hey-bearing and our legs are finally in a good rhythm, the tall-tree forest spits us onto the McKinley River Bar. The sky is gray, but the tippy top of the mountain is out above the clouds, as if she's peeking at us in a game of hide-and-seek. And the top of the mountain is beautiful, all shimmery, sparkly white — a little slice of hope against the stormy night sky.

The McKinley River runs in braids, small channels of water weaving together on the rocky bar. This river is much wider than the Savage; the gravel must stretch nearly a mile across before reaching the tundra on the far side.

There is no trace of humans except for a tripod — a landmark made out of three logs tied together in a teepee formation — to mark the place where the trail meets the river. Dad would have encountered this tripod on his way back to Wonder Lake after climbing the mountain.

Sophie scans the river, the glimmering stretches of water that weave across the gravel. Pretty to look at, but difficult to cross.

"Lily," she says, "this is *not* going to be easy."

She's right. I know how deep the water can be and how cold and fast-moving.

But crossing the McKinley River is the only way to get to Dad.

CHAPTER 20

Sophie doesn't say anything while we eat granola bars beside the river. She stares at the braids of glacier water and holds her silver feather up to her chin. We both know how Dad feels about river crossings. He always says they are the most dangerous thing in Denali Park, worse than bears and mountains and crevasses — worse because water channels are so cold, murky, and unpredictable. Water so cold you can get hypothermic in a matter of seconds. If you take a misstep, you can get swept away.

My whole plan feels cold, murky, and unpredictable now. It would be much nicer to be curled up in my sleeping bag tonight and not dealing with this river.

I try to push away thoughts of sleep. If I were asleep, what would that do to save Dad?

To finish off our midnight snack, Sophie and I move on to apples. After Sophie chews her apple down to the core, she stands up and hoists her pack onto her shoulders. I choke down the last of my apple and follow her lead.

We pace back and forth along the gravel bar for a while, looking for the best place to cross. Every other time I've crossed rivers in Denali, I've linked arms with Dad to help steady my steps. Linking arms with Sophie won't be so steady. She's got her green sneakers on too, and their rubber bottoms have a slippery tread.

"Up here!" I yell to Sophie. I have a spot, not too narrow, not too wide. It's impossible to tell exactly how deep it is, because the water is gray from glacier silt.

I pick up a rock and throw it into the river to evaluate depth.

Plop. Hard to tell, but definitely shouldn't be deeper than I am tall.

Sophie joins me. "This is a bad idea," she says.

I shake my head no. It can't be bad. It's the only way to the mountain.

Take it slow. Don't panic. I hear Dad's river-crossing words.

I loosen my backpack straps.

"We're really doing this?" Sophie asks, but she knows it's real, because she's rolling up her pant legs. No point rolling up mine. The water will come at least up to my knees.

We keep our shoes on because every little bit of grip on the river bottom helps.

"Ready?" I call over the McKinley River rush. I stare at the top of the mountain, not down at the water.

"Yes," Sophie says. We link arms, and mine trembles against hers.

"One, two, three, go!" I say.

The first step is the worst. The water fills my boot like liquid ice. The cold numbs my skin all the way through to the bone. Sophie pulls me closer with her linked arm, like the cold has gripped her, too.

The second step is a little bit better.

The river slaps against my shins, but I focus on the far side. On the third step, the water comes up above my knees. My knees!

"Almost across this braid," Sophie shouts over the rush of the water, and she's right, but it doesn't feel like it. We keep stepping. The water is almost up to my waist now.

I breathe in and out slowly, and my head spins from the icy grip of the river. *Look up, not down, Lily.* I hear Dad's words.

"Two more steps," I say, convincing myself that two steps is nothing.

The water shallows, and Sophie tugs a final tug and I'm back on the rocks.

"Phew," I say, but as soon as I say it, the relief turns back into fear. We've crossed one section of the river, but we're not even close to the other side. We're on a little patch of gravel, and we'll have to cross three or more braids before reaching safe ground.

Figuring out where to cross is the hard part. Sophie and I pace along the rocks again and look for the next best channel. The narrow ones are tempting, because they're an easy stone's throw across — but the problem is that they're usually deeper.

Sophie and I settle for a medium-length crossing. It should only be six or seven steps if we do it well.

"Ready, set, go!" I say, and we link arms for the second crossing.

No big deal. The water doesn't even come up to our knees. Between the second and third braids, Sophie and I teeter on a tiny sliver of rocky shore. We don't get to choose where to cross next. We have only two options: to move forward or to move back. It's easy to decide what we need to do — press on — but harder to take that first step back into the water.

Sophie squeezes my arm. "Let's go for it," she says.

Halfway across the third braid, the sky starts spinning above me. My legs are so cold that I'm losing my balance and my ability to will my body forward.

"Keep coming," Sophie says, and she tugs on my arm.

I drag my numb legs along, focusing on the far shore — and I get there.

"Sophie, I need a break," I say when we reach the rocks.

"Why?" she asks.

"I can't feel my legs."

She chuckles nervously. "Me either."

I rub my hands together and jog in place to try to bring feeling back to my toes and calves and knees. Sophie paces back and forth on our little stretch of shore. She's scouting our next and final crossing.

"If we can get across this, we'll be on our way," Sophie says.

But *this* — forging across one more stretch of glacier water — feels impossible. My legs are like ice cubes.

I glance down at my watch: one thirty a.m.

What idiots cross rivers at this hour? The daylight makes it appear okay, but not even daylight is strong enough to help us ford glacial rivers in the middle of the night.

"Ready?" Sophie asks.

"Not yet," I say over the rush of the water. I have never felt this *un*ready. Shivers zip through my wet body. Wet is not what I'd like to be right now.

I look toward the mountain, but the top no longer peeks out from the storm clouds. It hits me: If I'm cold, how cold is Dad?

"Let's go," I say to Sophie. Dad keeps me going.

The first three steps are normal. The current is swift, but the cold doesn't feel as cold because my legs are numb. On the fourth step, when I put my right boot down, a rock turns on the river bottom. I try to catch myself with my left foot, but the river current tips me over. I don't have time to scream. I hit the water, pulling Sophie down with me.

River water everywhere, sucking me under.

Ice cold.

I choke on water and gasp for air.

I can't see Sophie. All I can see is how fast the land is moving by. "Help!" I scream, but there's no help here. The shore is close, but my backpack catapults me downriver.

Dunk. My head goes under, and the weight of the pack drags me down.

Air. I need air.

I gasp for it, and I get a mouth full of water. I'm choking and spluttering, flipping through the ice water. I'm tossed by the river, and it's hard to feel up and down or side to side, but then I hear Dad's words: *Never ever give up on hope.*

I slip out of my backpack straps just in time to bob up to the surface for air.

I get it this time — a gulp of hope.

I'm tossed on my belly, then my back, but at least I have air.

Then I wash up on the rocky river bar, skidding on the gravelly shore. I shimmy my body up on the sharp rocks, choking. I grip the shore with my fingers to avoid getting swept back down.

I look at the river channel just in time to see my backpack — a speck — whip around the corner and disappear.

Sophie. Where is Sophie?

I look upriver, and she's not there. Downriver? No.

I choke for breath. Where *is* Sophie? I'm cough-
ing and shivering, but it's thinking about Sophie that
makes it worse.

Where is she? Have I lost her, too?

When I look upriver a second time, there she
is. Sophie. She's running down the gravel bar
toward me.

"Are you okay?" she asks. She's as soaked as I am.

"Yes," I say, but I don't feel okay. "What about you?"

Sophie sits down beside me on the rocks. "I thought
you were a goner, Lily," she says. We're shivering so hard
that we're having our own human-quakes.

"This was such a bad idea," she says.

I nod and shiver some more.

"Where's your pack?" Sophie asks.

"It's gone," I say, and that's when I start thinking
about it rushing downriver.

"Better than you or me," Sophie says, but I can tell
by the look on her face that she's thinking about our
lost food and gear.

What about Dad's map? I touch my vest pocket. It's
zippered shut. Good. I still have Dad's map, Dad's journal, my tiny flower book, my Sharpie, and my raven
feather. They're soggy now, but at least I have them.

Sophie rummages through her pack to find some dry clothes. The problem is that nothing is dry after a river plunge.

"What should we do?" I ask.

"I know one thing," Sophie says. "We're not crossing that river again right now."

Sophie and I huddle under her damp sleeping bag for a while. I'm tempted to start a fire, but fires aren't allowed in the backcountry of Denali National Park. Plus, my matches are gone, floating downriver in my pack. We couldn't start a fire even if we needed to.

I should have been more careful when I packed our bags. Good mountaineers know to split up all the essentials between backpacks — just in case you lose a pack or get separated from your partner.

Doubt creeps in slowly at first, and then it rushes into me, taking over along with the shivers.

"You don't think we're going to die out here, do you?" I ask Sophie.

"We better not," she says. "Mom will kill us."

"Very funny," I say, but talking about getting killed isn't funny at all after everything that has happened.

It's almost two a.m. Home sounds pretty good right now, but home without Dad is not home at all.

CHAPTER 21

Sophie and I sit in a shivery huddle. Dad's words play in my mind: *The only thing worse than being cold, wet, and hungry in the wilderness is to be in a hurry.*

We're really in trouble now. All strikes against us.

Shivering burns extra calories, so shivering isn't going to help. Warming up is essential, and we need to do it quickly. We only have one sleeping bag, a rain tarp, one ration of lunch, a can of pepper spray, Dad's rescue bag, and a clock ticking as fast as the current of the river.

"Let's get a move on," I say. Movement will help.

Sophie squeezes me tight. "Yes. Onward," she says. She's knows it's true — that we need to keep going.

"I'm glad it was your pack and not mine," Sophie says while she's rummaging through her gear.

"Thanks a lot," I say.

"No, it's because..." Sophie says, and she pulls something out of her pack.

"What?" I ask.

"I wasn't going to show you these until later," she says, teeth chattering. "But while we're stopped here, I might as well." She pulls out a brown paper bag and tosses it to me.

I flip over the bag. Two model birch-bark canoes slip out onto the rocks.

"How do you have these?" I ask. No doubt, these are Dad's birch-bark canoes.

"They were on his workbench in the garage," Sophie says. "I think he made them for us to race this summer when he returned from the mountain."

I can't believe Sophie found Dad's model canoes. Every summer, Dad spends days gathering bark and soaking spruce roots in the creek near home. Then he laces the bark into canoes for our races. He makes them watertight by melting tree sap onto the seams of the boats.

Dad says that making things with his hands helps him write stories in his mind — and then on paper for his newspaper column.

I hold a canoe up to my nose. Mmm. Fresh and woodsy. The smell of Dad and words and hope.

"We should race them," Sophie says.

"But then . . . they'll be gone forever," I say. That's the thing about Dad's model canoes. They're beautiful, but once you set them in the river, they disappear for good.

"He made them for us to race, Lily."

"I know, but I don't want to lose them."

"Maybe on the trip back?" Sophie asks.

I nod. Yes, by then we'll have Dad to help us, and he'll be able to make us more canoes when he gets home.

Sophie lays out all the contents of our lunch bag on the river bar: four peanut butter and jelly sandwiches on pilot bread, two bags of gummy bears, four fun-size Snickers, and a bag of trail mix. Not much fuel to get us to the mountain and back, but it will have to do.

"What are we going to do about our food?" Sophie asks.

"Ration it," I say. What else is there to do?

I wish the blueberries were ripe. Or that I'd put extra candy in my pockets.

Rationing candy makes me extra nervous.

Sophie shakes her head when she lays out Dad's rescue supplies. "Food would be a lot more useful than all this," she says, eyeing the rope and crampons.

"We lost both water bottles too," I say, changing the subject. "They were in my pack."

Sophie smiles. "Good thing Dad made his canoes watertight."

Yes. Model canoes will make perfect cups.

"You think there are beavers around here?" Sophie asks, and I know why she's asking.

"I hope not," I say, and take a long swig of water from the stern of my model canoe. Beaver fever. Giardia. Dad got the illness a few summers ago from drinking unfiltered water. He was miserable, running to and from the bathroom for weeks. The only way to prevent beaver fever is to filter, boil, or put purification tablets in the water. We have none of those three options today. There's not much to do but drink the water — and hope.

Hope. We've been doing a lot of that. I'm not sure it's helping, but I'm not about to stop. Dad better be right that hope knocks the socks off fear. Especially since I can't eat my way to the mountain with candy anymore.

I pull out Dad's map. There's a tiny star in a circle next to the McKinley River. I guess that was Dad's warning — a circled star means danger. I trace my finger up to the next star. It's a sloppy star in Dad's signature scrawl. Turtle Hill. There's no circle around it, so I think it's just a place where Dad spent the night.

Yes. I flip to his journal entry from Turtle Hill, and this is what it says.

> TURTLE HILL:
> NO BETTER FEELING IN THE WORLD THAN MY BACKPACK PACKED AND THE MOUNTAIN IN FRONT OF ME. SOFT TUNDRA SLEEPING ON TURTLE HILL TONIGHT.

"Let's try to get to Turtle Hill before we nap," I say. There's something nice about going to Dad's camp spot. It sounds safer there, like if Dad was once there, we'll be okay too.

"Sure," Sophie says, but I see the tired in her eyes, and I hope it's not too much farther.

CHAPTER 22

Sophie stops to retie her sneakers on a tundra knoll above the river bar, and that's when I see it: a gray animal moving along the rocks below.

At first I think it's a caribou.

But it's not.

I grab Sophie's binoculars from the top flap of her pack and zoom in.

"Wolf," I whisper. Just saying the word gives me goose bumps.

"Yeah, right," Sophie says, knowing how rare it is to see a wolf.

But it is a wolf. I trace his path and his slow, easy trot. He wears a thick, scruffy gray coat, and his nose swings low to the ground.

I follow his path with the binoculars and wonder: What has he seen out here? Did he watch us fall in the river, or is he just passing through?

It's a beautiful sort of silence — Sophie and me standing statue-still on the tundra, watching the lone wolf. He's just below us now, and I lose track of him when he comes to the edge of the tundra bank.

There for a while, and now gone.

I'm starting to think the wolf has trotted away into the night, but then the tundra rustles, and I know he's close.

I see his gray face first, shaggier and scruffier than the binocular view. Golden eyes. He stops and whimpers once — the first of us to speak.

Just as quickly as our eyes connect, the wolf turns and lopes back down to the river.

"He must not think we're a threat," Sophie whispers.

"I think he's a messenger."

I lie back against the tundra for a quiet moment. I squeeze my eyes shut to try to remember the scene. I need to describe it — every little magical detail — to Dad when I find him.

Easy trot. Golden eyes. One whimper.

There's something about the wolf that makes me feel so much closer to Dad.

CHAPTER 23

R eady to go?" Sophie asks, interrupting my reverie. I'm not ready to move on, but I know we must. The clock doesn't stop ticking, even for a wolf.

Blisters on my big toes sting as my wet feet rub against wet socks in wet boots. My body aches all over. Staying up all night is the least of it. Powering forward into morning without food is when the real exhaustion sets in. Sophie must feel the same way, because she doesn't bother to bend over and retie her sneaker laces, and she's limping.

A flash of worry crosses my mind when I think of Ranger Collins. Will she look for us before her hike? If she notices we're gone, then what?

"Keep. Eyes. Open," I say as I walk. Several times I land on my knees on the trail when I fall asleep on my feet.

Gear. Tallying up my gear will keep me awake. What exactly was in my backpack?

1) All the food, except for our lunch bag.
2) My sleeping bag.
3) Extra set of dry clothes.
4) Two pairs of dry socks.
5) Camp stove and fuel.
6) Matches.
7) Two water bottles.
8) Knife.

Ugh.

"Can I take your pack for a while?" I ask Sophie. Maybe if I carry the gear, I will feel more prepared. Maybe the weight of the pack will keep me awake.

"No," Sophie says, and I get it. The backpack is her only security.

We bushwhack our way up Turtle Hill. Sophie might say that Dad's dead, but that stride in her gait makes me wonder what she really believes.

"Do you think Dad knows we fell in the river?" I ask.

"Maybe," she says, "but I hope not. Dad always says ninety-nine percent of wilderness accidents are preventable."

"Yeah, but we're still alive, aren't we? He'd be proud of us for that." As I say it, I wonder: Would Dad be proud? I also wonder about his 99 percent rule. Was his fall on the glacier preventable? Where was his rope?

Talking to Sophie takes my mind off my blistered toes, my wet and tired body, and my increasingly grumbling belly. Sophie and I vow not to eat any food until lunchtime. But it's only six thirty a.m. now, and I'm not sure I'll make it until then.

I can't stop wondering about the rope. If Dad had been roped, he would be fine. Why would he have been so reckless?

The top of Turtle Hill isn't a grand destination, but we find a trail there — a real trail that leads from Turtle up to McGonagall Pass and the base of the mountain.

A trail is just what we need for quick and easier travel, and it's reassuring to know we've arrived at Dad's camp spot.

Dad put a tiny star on the map for a reason.

I curl up in the tundra and push away the things that I know are true: Time is the enemy when

1) you're wet,
2) you're hungry, and
3) you have many miles to go.

Yes, we qualify for all three.

But sleep feels more important than anything right now — more important than warmth, food, and the miles that separate us from Dad. Sophie sets her watch for our thirty-minute catnap. When we wake up, we'll press on.

Sophie shakes me. "Time to get going," she says.

I force my eyes open, and that's when I realize how cold I am. Beyond goose bumps and shivers. Cold on the outside and deep on the inside.

"You warm?" I ask Sophie.

"Not exactly sweating," she says, stealing a line from Dad. "Too cold to sleep."

I pull my body upright. The hunger lump in my stomach is like a jagged stone scratching at my insides.

"Twenty jumping jacks. Go!" Sophie says. She's right. Jumping jacks are the quickest way to warm up.

I start my twenty jumping jacks, and blood begins rushing back through my body, but the stone of hunger worsens. I'm really, really hungry. I've never been this hungry because I always pack extra food — and candy.

As I do the last two jacks, I notice Sophie sitting on the tundra changing her socks. When she pulls off the wet socks, her feet are bloody and swollen.

"What happened?" I ask.

"Blisters," she says, and pulls a fresh pair of socks right over her bloody feet.

"Why didn't you tell me?" I ask, and I can't believe how bad they are.

"What were you going to do, Lily?"

She has a point, but at least I could have felt sorry.

She continues: "Plus, I know better than to wear my high-tops out here." Sophie crams her feet back into the shoes, reminding me how tough she used to be. How tough she is becoming again.

Being out here has brought back that old tundra-loving Sophie I haven't seen in a while.

"Onward," Sophie says, and we set off. Progress is the only thing that feels useful, but the trail from Turtle Hill is muddy and brushy and slow going.

I would pay twenty dollars for a cheeseburger with fries right now. Fifty dollars, even. Heck, I'd pay sixty dollars if I could get a milkshake, too — a strawberry one with whipped cream and sprinkles on top.

I hear the water before I see it.

"We don't have another crossing, do we?" Sophie asks.

"Yes," I say, inspecting the rushing water. I've known it was coming for a while, but I pushed the knowledge to that part of my mind where the words *dead, crevasse,* and *gone* live.

I unfold Dad's map and, sure enough, he put a tiny star next to Clearwater Creek. A star with a dark circle around it.

Sophie sits down on a rock beside the water, stalling.

I flip open Dad's journal, and on page three there's a clue:

CLEARWATER CREEK CROSSING HARDER THAN McKINLEY. WATER UP TO MY KNEES. SHOULD HAVE WAITED UNTIL EARLY MORNING WHEN WATER IS LOWEST.

Great. What could be worse than our McKinley River crossing?

"Soph, I don't want to cross this creek right now," I say. Actually, I don't want to cross the creek ever, but especially not now. My nylon pants are finally starting to dry, I'm slightly warm, and all I want to do is eat or sleep or both. We've been at it for more than twelve hours straight, and it's almost noon.

Sophie motions for the journal, and I hand it over.

She reads slowly and then says, "We better follow Dad's advice. Let's get across the river while it's technically still morning and the water's low."

"What about sleep?" I ask, feeling the pull of it.

"We can sleep when we're dead," Sophie says. It's another one of Dad's lines, but I really don't like thinking about dead.

Sophie's still carrying the pack, but she doesn't strap it tight across her chest for this crossing. She must want an easy escape if she falls in the creek. I don't have my pack anymore, of course, but I turn Sophie's sleeping bag stuff sack into a makeshift pack. I feel safer with a pack, like the extra weight will keep me stitched onto the earth. I carry two of the fun-size Snickers in my pocket, just in case we get separated. Spare candy is my only backup survival plan.

My boots are finally damp instead of drenched, but I leave them on for the crossing. It's worth it to have extra grip on the creek bottom.

"Ready?" Sophie asks. I don't feel one bit ready.

"One, two, three, go!" she says.

Sophie holds on to my arm so tight that I'm afraid she's going to pull me over. Pull me in.

The water is bone-numbing cold, just like the McKinley River: a shock to the body.

Slow and methodical. The first two steps are only calf-deep, but on the third step I yell, "Ack!" as my foot reaches for the creek bottom. My body tips to the right, but I reach bottom in time to steady myself.

"It's okay," Sophie says, but I can tell by her grip that she's not certain we're okay.

The fourth and fifth steps knock the breath out of me — the cold water flash-freezing my bones — but I focus on the far shore.

The dizzying cold brings back Dad's words: "Stay calm, Lily. Calm chases away fear." Dad's voice is real. Real until Sophie yanks my arm. "Keep coming. Keep *on* coming, Lily," she says.

I'm stepping and the cold water is gripping and the sky is spinning, but I keep on going because Sophie's tugging on my arm. When we reach the far bank, I'm relieved to plant my boot up onto the tundra. Even if Dad isn't here waiting for me.

"Why did the chicken cross the road?" Sophie asks. Dad loves chicken-crossing-the-road riddles.

"To get to the other side," I say, not really in the mood for riddles.

"Why did we cross the creek?" Sophie asks.

"I don't know," I say, but I *do* know why.

"To get to Dad's mountain," she says. I nod, because she's right. But I'm shocked, too: Has Sophie become a believer? Is she looking for Dad — real Dad — too?

I unlace my hiking boots, pull them off, and dump out the water. I don't bother trying to wring out my socks or pants. It's too cold to dry out anything today. It must be about thirty-five degrees — not cold enough to become ice, but darn close.

"Let's set up a catnap spot," Sophie says.

Phew. Sleep at last.

I build a mattress out of willows, piling up branches to create a nest above the wet tundra. I do it just how Dad taught me. I lay out Sophie's sleeping bag, and I imagine my own, still floating down the McKinley River. Then I cover Sophie's lone sleeping bag with our rain tarp. It will have to do for both of us.

Even though sleep sounds good, we can't resist food any longer. Before lying back against our willow mattress, we have to snack on something. Sophie and I agree to eat *only* one peanut butter and jelly sandwich each. I make mine last ten minutes. Mouse-size bites combined with sips of water from my birch-bark canoe make the food seem larger than its actual size. I can almost believe I've just eaten a full meal.

I'm exhausted, but falling asleep is still impossible. I'm shivery, wet, and hungry, and willow branches poke up through my damp long johns and into my back. Sophie and I lie huddled together, two cold caterpillars trying to stay warm underneath our one mummy bag and rain tarp.

"You warm?" Sophie asks.

"No," I say.

"Warm enough?" she asks, and I know exactly what she's asking.

"Yeah. I'm not going to die from this amount of cold."

"Good. Me either," she says. "Good night."

The drizzly rain is loud against the tarp. But if we can just get a few hours of good sleep, maybe we can muster the energy to get to Dad by evening.

CHAPTER 24

Iwake up curled in a tight ball, shivering, with no mummy bag on top of me. My hands are over my head the way my teacher taught me to duck and cover in an earthquake. I think the nightmare came back, but I'm too cold to be sure.

I know one thing: We're close to Dad — maybe seven miles, give or take a little — and I can't get the wolf and the golden eyes and the whimper out of my mind.

I stand up and pace around the tundra to warm up. I'm wearing every last piece of clothing I have. Sophie doesn't budge from beneath her sleeping bag, which she has hogged all to herself. She's all warm and wrapped up in it. When she breathes, a puff cloud rises into the cold air.

I jog to the edge of the creek and fill up my canoe with water to drink. Then I do forty-five jumping jacks. On the thirtieth, I feel my feet again. By the fortieth, my legs are no longer numb.

As my body awakens to the day, so does the memory of our river plunge. The wet, toppling and choking — and water everywhere.

And the clock is still ticking. Dad's been missing for six days now.

Six days!

We need to get a move on.

"Sophie, Sophie," I say, shaking her cocoon. I feel bad for waking her back into this hungry, cold, and no-trace-of-Dad-yet world. But we have to keep on moving if we're going to change that.

Sophie peeks her head out of the bag.

"What time is it?" she asks.

"Time to go — *now*," I say. Clock time doesn't matter. We're on Dad time — mountain time.

Sophie wakes up as clumsily as a ground squirrel stumbling out of hibernation. "I have to eat something before we start out," she says. When she swaps her socks, I notice that the blisters on her toes are ballooning up even more. I don't know how she can fit her feet

132

into her sneakers. Plus, the sneakers are hardly lime green anymore, scuffed and smudged with trail grit.

Sophie's a trooper, and I can already imagine what Dad will do when he sees her out here. He'll give Sophie a pat on the back and say, *Way to get those feet back to the mountains and your head back to the wild air.* And Sophie will say those words that she really needs to say: *I love you, Dad.*

We divvy up our only bag of trail mix. I eat it one food type at a time: ten peanuts, three almonds, nine M&M's, two cashews, and fourteen raisins. Why are there always more raisins than the good stuff? Raisins are just filler food. I could eat hundreds of M&M's right now.

I gulp one more canoe full of creek water and tally up our remaining food supply: four fun-size Snickers, two bags of gummy bears, and two soggy PB&J sandwiches on pilot bread.

How far can two girls get on these rations?

Reading my mind, Sophie answers. "The longer we wait, the worse it's going to be."

"Darn right," I say.

If we've learned one thing so far on this trip, it's not to dilly-dally and think too much about food. But right now, for some reason I can't stop thinking about that green bean casserole that Barb brought to the house a few days ago. Which leads me to start thinking about her story of Moses dying on a mountain.

CHAPTER 25

Things start feeling better as we walk away from our sleep spot. We're close to McGonagall Pass — the base of Denali. No more big river crossings, and we're not far from Dad's stash of peaches and brandy. With any luck, Dad will be there too.

A breeze picks up — and it meets me head-on. The breeze is not like the one in the Irish blessing song that Dad loves so much, the one with the lyric "May the wind be always at your back." Nope. Today the wind is blowing right smack into our faces.

But we're so close. We can't let wind slow us down now.

It doesn't matter that my feet are sloshing around inside my boots, or that I'm hungry — ravenous, as

Dad would say. I'm so focused on the ground directly in front of my boots that I don't see the brown beast until it's pretty close.

Galloping toward us.

"Sophie!" I say.

"Bear!" she confirms.

I unclip the pepper spray from Sophie's pack. My hands are shaky and jerky, but my mind says *hurry-hurry-hurry*.

"Whoa!" I scream.

"He's coming!" Sophie yells.

"Hey!" I wave my arms, but the grizzly doesn't stop, and he's huge.

Sophie drops to the ground to play dead. Just like she's supposed to.

I stand frozen, unable to move.

"Drop!" Sophie says.

I expect him to veer off. Bears don't usually charge all the way, but he's almost here.

I yank on the safety latch of the pepper spray. Ugh. It's not coming off.

I yank harder. *Pop!*

It's off. Just in time. The grizzly is here. Eyes huge. Fur raised up on his neck. He stops just a few feet away and stands up on his hind legs, and just as soon as he's up on two — pausing for a breath — he's back down on all fours coming closer.

"Hey! Whoa!" I holler one last time, but then I step in front of Sophie and press down hard on the button. *Pshhhhhhh.*

It all happens so fast.

I see shadows and hear grunts.

Bear. Spray. *Smack.* Sting.

My eyes burn and everything gets blurry. The air is thick and peppery and impossible to breathe. The huge brown shadow goes from large to medium to smaller. But everything is silent — slow panic silent — with eyes on fire.

"Lily, Lily," Sophie says. "Are you okay?"

"I don't know," I say, and my heart is racing through questions: *What happened? Where's the bear? Why are my eyes on fire?*

"He's gone," Sophie says, and that's when I realize that the spray did it — fended off the bear.

I cough and cough, and panic rises. I can hardly see anything.

"Did he get you?" I ask.

"No. I'm okay," Sophie says. "What about you?"

I'm rubbing my eyes, the sting so sharp I wonder if I'll ever be able to see again.

"Sophie, what happened to my eyes?" I say, but it's becoming clear: the wind. That dratted wind blew pepper spray into my eyes.

"Can I help?" Sophie asks. I manage to force one eye open for a second.

"Yow!"

"Hold on," Sophie says. "Let me read the pepper spray canister." But I'm worried about the bear now too. Where did he go? Will he come back for us? Is he circling around?

After a minute or so, Sophie says, "If I rinse your eyes with water, you'll be okay."

"So I'm not going to be blind?" I ask.

"Doesn't sound like it," Sophie says.

"What about the bear? Is he gone?"

"No trace," says Sophie, and I hope she's right. "But hold on. I'll be right back. I need to go find water."

Sophie returns with canoes filled with water from a nearby kettle pond, one of the glacier-formed lakes on the tundra. It stings when she pours water into my eyes, but vision begins to come back — vision and the reality that we've had more than a few close calls.

"We never should have come out here," I say. "If you had died, I'd never forgive myself."

"Well, I didn't die," Sophie says, "and there's no way we're turning back now." She's hugging me, and I don't want it—the hug—to end. "It's not your fault, Lily. Plus, we were just in the bear's way. He didn't want to eat us."

"It *is* my fault. I made you come all the way out here," I say.

Sophie holds me in the hug, but I'm still panicky inside. "No, Lily. I agreed to come." She squeezes me like old times.

"Plus, you did it," she says.

"What?" I ask.

"Saved me with the pepper spray."

I hug Sophie harder, but I don't feel like I've saved anything.

"We're not going to give up on Dad's mountain just yet," Sophie says, "and that's final."

CHAPTER 26

Sophie leads, and I'm following close behind her.

"We deserve these," she says, opening our second to last bag of gummy bears.

I eat three gummy bears from the package and then stop. It's wrong to eat them when they don't even taste good.

"Aren't you scared?" I ask.

"Sure, I'm scared," Sophie says. "But what can I do about it?"

"You finish these bears," I tell Sophie, and pass her the package. Giving away my gummy bears feels like *doing* something.

We walk for hours, and we don't bother making noise anymore. What are the chances of getting chased by a bear twice in one day?

For a while, I sense something following us. I think it's the bear at first, but the noises are wispier, like the sounds of a small animal. I'm convinced that it's the wolf, but when I turn around, he's not there. Maybe all that pepper spray has made me crazy.

Somewhere near the top of the pass, I muster up some new energy and go by Sophie. I don't have dry socks or a proper amount of candy, but we're almost to Dad, and I have enough hope to take the lead.

CHAPTER 27

I've never doubted the scale of the mountain, but when we reach the top of McGonagall Pass, it really hits me. She's huge, mostly white, with dark rough patches where the wind has whipped snow off her face. Denali. She's so big that I have to arch my neck back to see the bright blue of the sky. Yes. The sky's blue now. I'm not quite sure when the drizzle ended.

We're finally here. At the base of the mountain. The place where Dad left his stash.

I scan the tundra. Nothing obvious. No pot of gold. No X to mark the spot. No Dad. A lone arctic ground squirrel pokes his head up from a nearby hole. "Cheep, cheep, cheep."

"Where is he?" I whisper.

The Muldrow Glacier is an ice and snow ribbon winding its way up the mountain. Is Dad in there?

I shake my head no, pushing away the thought of Dad trapped in the ice.

He's not.

He's up here — out here — somewhere.

Sophie reaches the top of the pass seconds later. We don't talk. I pull the binoculars from the top flap of her pack. I zoom in on the glacier ice, the snout of Denali. I always thought ice was just one color, but this ice is white, blue, green, and gray, depending on how the light falls on each glimmering stretch.

No sign of Dad in the colors.

"We made it," Sophie says, and she hugs me from behind.

"Where is he?" I ask.

"Oh, Lily," she says.

"Where?"

"He's not here," she says, her words like quills in me, barbs digging deep beneath my skin.

"He has to be."

"He's not," Sophie says, and she's clutching her silver feather like it's the only thing left.

"So that's it, then?" I ask. "You give up?"

"Getting here is something," Sophie says. "In fact, it's a lot."

"I wouldn't have walked all this way just to get here," I say. "I need Dad, too."

Sophie swings the pack off her shoulders and sits down on a tundra patch. She lies back, props her head up on a rock, and closes her eyes.

"How can you just lie there?" I say. "This is no time for a nap." There are tremors running through me, and I can't still them.

"I need a moment," Sophie says. A tear slides down her right cheek, and it — the tear — makes me furious.

"You need a moment for *what*? We found *nothing*," I say.

"I know," Sophie says. "That's just it. It takes time to soak in the nothing — and remember." As she says these words, her hope flies away into the high mountain air.

"No, no, *no*," I say. I gasp for breath. "We can't give up now."

Sophie doesn't budge from her spot on the tundra.

"I thought you were a believer," I say.

"He's not here, Lily . . . and he's not coming, either."

"What about his stash, then?"

"I'll help you look for it, but first I need some alone time."

"We've been *alone* without him the whole trip," I say. "What we need is to be *together* again."

"Not going to happen," Sophie says. But it will, it will, it will.

What I do next is wrong in every way. I pull our food bag from Sophie's pack, walk away from her, and start eating. I begin with the four remaining fun-size Snickers. I pace around as I eat, hunting for clues. Surely food will help me figure this out.

When the Snickers are gone, I gobble the last two peanut butter and jelly sandwiches. My mouth is so dry the peanut butter sticks to my teeth and my tongue, but I don't care. I simply chew, swallow fast, and keep on eating.

Food is momentum. One foot in front of the other. No stopping. No giving up.

Soon I've eaten everything except for the last bag of gummy bears.

I focus my eyes on the ground beneath my feet rather than on the mountain looming above me. There must be a sign of Dad somewhere. I skim the tundra.

For the stash.

Footprints?

Candy wrappers?

Any trace of him?

Nothing.

"Dad," I whisper into the air, and I wave my arms as if something or someone might be looking down on me.

It's the empty feeling in my chest that's the worst: Could it be that Dad's not here? That I won't ever find him?

No, Lily. Don't let hope fly away.

Where is his stash? I pull out his map. There's a star right where I'm standing, but definitely no stash. Maybe Dad crawled his way out of the glacier and collected his peaches and brandy. But then why wouldn't he have come home?

The Muldrow Glacier haunts me, her slick snow and ice glimmering under the sun like an evil finger wagging at me. I trace the glacier on the map. Dad put a circled star on the Muldrow, so why didn't he rope up?

Mom told me that the place where he fell was usually no problem. Easy. Close to the end of the climb — and there were usually no crevasses there.

I know what to do next.

I go back to Sophie's pack and pull out a few pieces of Dad's rescue gear: a rope and a pair of crampons.

"Soph," I say.

No answer. She's either asleep or just plain ignoring me.

She doesn't know that I just ate all our food, and she doesn't need to know what I'm going to do next. This wasn't part of my plan, exactly. But I was sure Dad would be here at the base of the glacier.

Now I'm going to have to walk up the glacier to find him.

CHAPTER 28

First things first: I scramble down the rocky hill to get to the tongue of the glacier. Halfway down, I try to scree ski through the rocks, but there's no way to glide. I slip, topple, and slam into the gravelly hill.

My butt lands hard against the rocks, and I start skidding again down the slope. The scree isn't like powder snow. It's rough, and the sharp rocks spit me down the hill.

Thud. The hard landing knocks the breath out of me. It's a lot like getting washed up on the McKinley River bar. I don't quite know whether to feel lucky to be alive or terrified by what might have happened.

But this is no time to dally. I hoist my body up to sitting position and assess the damage. I can still lift my head. There's no blood, and my boots are still tied on my feet.

Phew.

Just in front of me, one boot step away, is the Muldrow Glacier.

"Dad!" I yell up the mountain of ice.

Silence.

I bend over and secure Dad's crampons onto my feet. They're little metal spikes for my boots that help me grip the snow and ice. They're much too big for me, loosely fitting onto my boots, but they're better than nothing.

I start walking, one foot in front of the other. Glacier walking is slow, slippery, and cold, but I keep on going. It's good to be here on the glacier after thinking about it nonstop for almost a week.

A week. Dad's been missing almost a week.

I pull the last bag of gummy bears from my pocket, and the bears lead me up the glacier. It's a trance, these bears combined with this snow and ice. I eat one bear every ten steps, and the stepping is slow business. Like walking on my school ice rink, except it's a sloped rink. I scooch my boots along the slick ground and grip my toes to my insoles to keep balance. The crampons make a creaky sound on the ice — spooky.

Progress is unsteady. Some sections are glare ice, while others are punchy, wet snow. I'm unsure of how each step will be. I don't look up the slope. I focus only on the shifting ice and snow beneath my crampons, trying to keep my foothold.

Red bear. Ten steps. Green bear. Ten more steps. Yellow bear. The bears pile up in my stomach, and they cartwheel inside me. The glacier looks almost like water now — water swirling. That's what happens when you stare at snow and ice too long.

It's weird. This glacier is nothing like my nightmare. It's beautiful. Too beautiful to swallow up Dad.

But it's also massive.

The slope steepens, and that's when worry creeps in. There are crevasses here. Gaping holes, like the one that supposedly swallowed Dad. I'm not sure if you can always see them coming, or if they just gulp you up forever. Dad never taught me about crevasses, except I know that a rope can save you if you're in one. But you need a climbing partner to rope to, and Sophie's not here.

What keeps me moving is a flash of red tape ahead.

The red tape is tied onto a couple of bamboo wands used as trail markers. It's only a few yards now.

Is it Dad's stash?

A sign?

I try to speed up my walking, but each step is steeper and more treacherous than the one before. When I can't stand up anymore, I kneel on the ice and grip it with my hands and toe tips. I crawl — inch by inch — up the glacier. Crawling brings back the nightmare, except crawling is hardly even possible on ice. It's more like slow scooching.

Finally, using the grip of the crampons, I manage to stand up and walk the last few steps to the red tape.

When I arrive, the crossed wands don't seem to mark anything at first. It's just red tape tied to two bamboo sticks.

But then I see words. There's a message scribbled in black ink on the red tape: *DANGER! Crevasse ahead.*

Could this be the one?

There's no way to tell, but when I look in front of

me at the gaping ice hole, I immediately see that it's a trap. The hole is massive and bottomless, with sheer ice on all sides.

Only a miracle could help someone out of this cavern.

I want to inch closer to the crevasse, to see if there's any sign of Dad down in it, but I can almost hear him whisper, "Don't make someone else's mistakes." No. I can't crawl toward an open crevasse unroped.

I sit cross-legged on the ice and read the message on the red tape again.

DANGER! Crevasse ahead.

I hold the red tape up to the mountain light and realize there's more writing on the flip side. Someone scribbled these words:

Rest in peace, dear Charley.

CHAPTER 29

D ad!" I yell. "Dad!"
   Silence.

Silence as empty as my bag of gummy bears. Silence as deep as the ice in front of me. I stare at the crevasse and take in the colors of the ice. When the white and gray and green and blue mix together and make me dizzy, I close my eyes and just breathe in and out, in and out.

"Dad," I whisper, one last time with my eyes shut, but I don't expect him to answer.

I know then that the silence will be long.

There's no way Dad crawled hundreds of feet up and out of this ice. The nightmare had made it seem possible, but seeing it now — the endless ice trap — I know there's no way.

This is his spot — his last one on earth.

I breathe in deeply, but there's not enough air to fill me. This is it.

When I open my eyes, I look above the crevasse to the trail coming down the mountain. I wonder what Dad's last steps felt like. Alone. Did his steps feel lonely?

Or was he just enjoying one of his favorite mountain days?

Did Dad's last step feel like his last step on earth, or his first step of a new adventure? Did he know when he was falling that it was his last mountain moment? Did he think of me?

I can't believe I'm letting myself think of Dad no longer stepping his way through life. But peering into the glacier is more real than the phone call. More real than the green bean casserole. More real than the river. Real because I know it for myself — step by step — that sometimes the mountain really does win.

I don't inch my way any closer to the crevasse, but I lean forward until my lips touch the cold glacier ice. When I kiss that ice, I feel it — mountain sense — and just how close I am to Dad.

It's not like his bear hug or a game of Scrabble. It's not like a gummy bear feast or canoe race or crossword puzzle in the morning. But I feel him — Dad — like he's perched on my shoulder on this mountain, keeping me stitched to the ice.

A cold breeze picks up, and it blows my dirty hair into my eyes. I pull my lucky raven feather from my vest pocket and smooth its crumpled threads. Then I tuck it into the knot of red tape.

I love you, Dad. Love, Lily, I write on the red tape, using Dad's Sharpie.

It doesn't look quite right until I add Sophie's name too.

Then I pull a few forget-me-nots from my flower book. I set the pressed flowers on the ice, and I hope Dad feels my tiny gift.

When I peer back down the glacier, I realize how far I've come. The ice path is shimmery, slippery, and haunting. The brightness of it — the sun reflected on ice — is blinding.

And my butt is wet from sitting cross-legged on ice.

It's time to get up and go, but it's hard to move. To get up and walk away from all that hope. All that mountain sense. All that Dad.

But I do get up, because Sophie's back on the pass and she doesn't know about Dad.

After a few steps backtracking, I realize that walking down ice is much trickier than walking up it.

I'm creeping down the glacier with Dad's screechy crampons, but it doesn't last long. Suddenly I'm slithering and sliding.

"Help!" I yell, and I hear it twice because voices echo on ice.

"Help!" I shout again. My head is below my feet, and I'm cartwheeling. The landscape is choppy — chunks of sky and ice and mountain all blurring.

It's the same as the river. The tipping and toppling.

I hit my head — and my right rib crunches — before skidding to a halt. The impact knocks the breath out of me.

"Youch," I say to the mountain air.

I'm not sure what I hit, but I'm still alive. Even if the jagged rocks make it hard to breathe, hard to think, and hard to move. I'm still here.

Face-down on the ice.

I lie still until the ice melts into my dirty long johns. The cold grips me, and it feels good, like a full-body ice pack.

When I turn over, the sky is still blue above me. I'm still here.

Dad's still gone.

CHAPTER 30

I scramble up the rocky slope to McGonagall Pass and collapse at the top. With every in-breath comes a sharp pain in my side. I put pressure on my rib cage, and breathing gets easier.

Anger builds inside me, and I can't fend it off. I make fists with each hand and pound them into the tundra: Why, why, why did Dad have to slither his way into a crevasse? Why couldn't he have roped up . . . or crawled out . . . or just stayed home?

Then he'd still be alive.

"Lily," Sophie says, running toward me. "What were you thinking, climbing up there?" She looks absolutely furious, with wide eyes and flushed cheeks.

"I had to go find him," I say.

157

"Great, and get yourself killed too?" she asks, and the panic in her voice is real.

"Yes, but I didn't," I say. "That's the important part. I'm still here."

"You better be," Sophie says, and I see the hurt in her eyes, and that's when I see what she's holding: a bucket. Dad's stash!

She kneels in front of me and dumps the contents of the bucket onto the tundra. I know right away that it's Dad's stash because *Charley* is written in Sharpie ink on both sides. The bucket is gnawed on, battered by teeth and claw marks — maybe by the grizzly that charged us? Or what about that wolf?

As promised by Dad's journal, there are two cans of peaches and a bottle of brandy inside. Sophie holds up the bottle of brandy to the sky like she might find clues or at least Dad's handprints. Then she picks up the two cans of peaches, one in each hand.

There's something else, too: a small drawstring bag.

I know what's in it without opening it.

Scrabble tiles.

Of course. Dad wanted to play Scrabble as soon as he got off the mountain. He never carried the board; he always built words straight onto the tundra.

Sophie loses it when she sees the tiles. Tears stream down her cheeks, and she doesn't bother wiping them away. She curls in on herself, knees up to her chest, and she's crying so hard that her pant legs are sopping. Dad's the word guy, and here is his unplayed game.

"Sophie, I found Dad's spot," I say.

"What spot?" she asks, but she doesn't lift her head from her sopping knees.

"You know, *the* spot, on the glacier," I say, pointing up the ice.

Sophie shakes her head and refuses to look *there*.

"Now I know," I say.

"Know what?" Sophie asks.

"He's not alive," I say, "and it's okay. I mean, it's not okay, but at least I know."

"What makes you sure?" Sophie asks.

"I found the crevasse — the place where Dad disappeared," I say. "It's huge. There's no way Dad crawled hundreds of feet to get out."

"Did you see him down in there?" Sophie asks. "How are you sure?" I see the pain — all that pain — of her not knowing with my same certainty. She must have kept a tiny thread of hope inside her.

"Trust me, Soph. He's really gone," I say, and I hate being the one to clip that last thread. That's what everyone else has been doing to me until now.

I pick up the drawstring bag and hand it to Sophie. "A game of Scrabble?" I ask.

"Yes," she says, "and let's break open the peaches, too."

We play Scrabble on the flattest patch of tundra we can find. It's midnight, but there's still dusky light. We build words right onto the tundra. At first it's weird to play Scrabble without Dad. But it's so much better than sitting around and thinking. And we're flat out of candy now, so at least Scrabble tiles push away my need for gummy bears.

We play for a long time — slowly and methodically like Dad always did. Between turns, Sophie and I gobble peaches. They are even tastier than I imagined.

When we get to the last few letters, I scatter them on the tundra for Dad. He would know just how to use the final letters to finish — and win — the game.

Seeing the words on the tundra makes me feel close to him.

"This trip hasn't been only bad," Sophie says, "except for the almost-dying parts."

"We still have a long way home," I say.

"Yeah, but on the bright side, we have another can of peaches," Sophie says.

"And a full bottle of brandy," I add, unscrewing the lid.

I take a swig. Ack. It's bitter.

Yuck!

I swallow, and then I feel it, the warmth inside my body. The warm part must be what Dad liked so much. The warm part helps me forget about the jagged rocks clawing through my rib cage.

I hand the bottle over to Sophie. She takes a short swig, and she must feel the warmth too.

"We're living like queens," she says, and it's true. Queens of Dad's mountain.

Sophie smiles, the first real smile I've seen in ages. She puts the cap back on the bottle and sets the brandy beside the letters we used — for Dad.

CHAPTER 31

Dear Dad,
I'm here at the base of the mountain. We found your stash and celebrated for you. Don't worry . . . we only tasted the brandy. We even played Scrabble. I'll pick up your journal from here. You never know, maybe I'll even climb your mountain someday — with Sophie. Time to go back to Mom.
Love, Lily

My hand shakes when I ink *Love, Lily*. Then I close Dad's journal and lie back against the damp tundra. A good feeling warms my insides. Being here at the mountain is something. No Dad. No miracles. No more food. But there's something about coming all this way that's good.

A reverie. That's what Dad calls it. Dreamy mountain sense.

It doesn't last long. Soon the reverie fades, and a new list of questions buzzes around in my mind like mosquitoes: *What will Mom say when she finds out that we came here? Does Ranger Collins know what we've done? How will I ever tell Jenny or go to school or think about Moses again?*

"I'm starved," Sophie says. "Can you get the food from our pack?"

Double drats. Sophie doesn't know that I ate all of it. What was I thinking? She agreed to come all the way out here, and then I eat all the food, and we're days from home.

"Eat some of these," I say, handing her the second can of peaches.

"No more peaches," Sophie says.

"It's all we've got," I say.

Sophie squints at me, but she's too tired to ask more questions.

I'm shivery and damp and too tired to fall asleep. The pain in my chest is constant.

I crawl over to our backpack and grab our one wet sleeping bag and the rain tarp. It's going to be a cold night. I give Sophie the sleeping bag, and then I wrap myself up in the tarp like a burrito.

I wake up shivering. Shivering hard. With every tremor in my body comes a sharp pain to my rib cage. I focus hard on each breath and try to remember what's happened. Dad's gone — really gone. I'm hurt and I ate all of our food, and Sophie doesn't know this yet.

It doesn't take much waking up to know we're in a lot of trouble now, and we're nearly twenty miles from home, with rivers to cross and no food to fuel the journey.

Sophie has the wet sleeping bag all to herself.

I'm cold, but not too cold to know that we need to act quickly.

Cold. Wet. Hungry. Injured. These are all recipes for a wilderness disaster.

I fold up the tarp.

It's time to go home. For me. For Sophie. For Mom. Especially for Dad.

I wrap Dad's rescue rope snug around my rib cage and then knot it off so it stays in place. Phew. I can breathe easier now with the pressure.

If only I could warm up.

I start a jumping jack. "Yow," I say. Pain needles its way through my rib cage. The rope might help stop my pain, but jumping jacks are too much.

"Never let a cold person go to sleep in the woods," Dad always said. "Hypothermia will let you slip away into forever sleep."

I didn't come all this way to die. And what about Sophie?

"Wake up, wake up," I say, and my chest hurts when I say it.

No reply.

"Sophie," I say again, and my heart races. What if she just slipped into forever sleep?

I sit up, clutching my ribs. "Sophie," I say one last time.

"Yeah?" She rolls over to face me.

"Time to get up — *now*," I say.

"I need more sleep," she says. "What are you doing?"

"Getting ready to go," I say, and I feel the rush of it in me — to finish the trip right.

Dad might have messed up when he decided not to use the rope. He might have been reckless the one time when it mattered most. But I know as sure as the mountain is beautiful that he'd want us to make it home safely now — for him and for Mom.

He would be mad as a wolverine if we gave up.

CHAPTER 32

L ily," a voice calls out, and I jump back.

"Hello," the voice calls again. I scan the tundra. Two humans walk toward us at the top of the pass. This voice stuns me out of my mountain world.

Then I see the hats. Ranger hats.

My head pounds and my stomach growls, but my rib and chest don't hurt as much. Not with the pressure of the rope.

"Is that you?" says the voice, and it's a woman, and she's close now.

I wave back.

She's close enough that I see it's Ranger Collins. She's peering up at me like I'm an apparition. Another ranger — the man ranger from the talk — stands beside her, but he doesn't say anything.

"Sophie, get up. Get up!" I say, shaking her mummy sleeping bag beside me.

"Huh?" Sophie asks.

"Wake up — the rangers are here." It can't be good that two park rangers walked all the way out here.

"You're delusional," Sophie says, and I agree: it sounds delusional.

"Not this time," I say. "This is for real."

Sophie sits up, shivering and slouched.

"I'm so glad you're here," Ranger Collins says, and I see the worry lines across her face.

"Why did you come all this way?" I ask, because what else do I say to her.

"I found your backpack washed up on the river bar," she says.

"So you thought we were dead?"

"I did at first," she says. "Then I used binoculars and spotted the two of you on the far side of the river, headed toward Turtle Hill."

"Did you call our mom?" Sophie asks.

"Yes, I had to call her," the ranger says.

"Did she freak out?" I ask.

"No. I just left a message on her phone."

"We're going to be grounded forever," Sophie says, and it's true.

"How did you know we'd be here at McGonagall?" I ask.

"Where else would you go? This is your dad's place."

Ranger Collins gets it. She knows exactly why we're right here, right now.

She kneels on the tundra. "What's the deal with the rope?" she asks, eyeing my makeshift rib brace.

"I took a tumble," I say, "and I think I have a broken rib. But it'll heal." The man ranger looks at me like I'm officially crazy.

"Are you two hungry?" Ranger Collins asks, like it's no big deal. "We brought sandwiches."

"Ravenous," I say, using Dad's word.

"We've been rationing big time," Sophie says.

"Until I gorged myself last night," I add.

"So *that's* why you wouldn't give me any food?" Sophie asks, her eyes wide.

"Sorry," I say, meaning it.

Ranger Collins pulls out a bag of food. Salami and cheese sandwiches have never looked so good.

"I have a story to tell you. It's about your dad," Ranger Collins says while we're scarfing down our sandwiches. "I talked to him at the beginning of the expedition. He came by the station with his climbing partner and their two monstrous backpacks. I invited them in for a cup of tea, and your dad settled in for a long while. I've never seen a man so excited to be headed for Denali."

I can see Dad's face now, and the way he would have grinned while holding a mug of hot tea.

Ranger Collins continues: "He told me this would be his last big climb for a while, so he wanted to enjoy every minute. Then he told me about his daughters, how they were the best in the world."

"Did he really say that?" Sophie asks.

"He said it more than once, and he told me you'd be back to Wonder Lake later this summer, all four of you."

Sophie's eyes brighten.

"He even had a photo of you two in his pocket. 'My lucky charms,' he called you when he showed me the picture."

Hearing the ranger talk about Dad reminds me how much he loved this mountain and how much he loved us. And it makes me happy to think he has — or had — a picture of us in his pocket while he climbed.

"Here," she says, pulling a thermos of tea from her pack. Sophie and I instinctively pull out our model canoes, and the ranger looks at us strangely.

"Our cups," I say.

She nods like of course they're our cups, and then she fills them with tea.

"To Dad," I say, and I click my canoe against Sophie's.

"I love you, Dad," Sophie whispers, and she whispers it like she believes Dad can hear. In that moment — when our canoes click — we both know it completely.

Dad's gone in some ways, but he's also here at this mountain.

With us.

And if Dad had to die somewhere, this mountain was a pretty good place.

"It's time to go," I say, and it's the readiest I've felt on the whole trip. The sun filters through low clouds, making McGonagall Pass misty and dreamlike.

"I'm ready this time," I say, and I mean it.

I'm ready for Mom's spaghetti and a hot bath. Ready for dry socks, carpet between my toes, clean sheets, and sleep. I'm even ready for the long walk home.

In a perfect world, Dad would be here too, but I know now he won't be.

"What about the Scrabble game?" Sophie asks, after she has crammed all our stuff into her pack.

"Let's leave it just like this," I say, peering down at the wooden Scrabble tiles built into words on the tundra — with extra letters scattered for Dad. Sophie holds her silver feather up to her lips and nods.

Then we turn toward Wonder Lake to head home.

CHAPTER 33

It's hard to walk away from the mountain. Every time I glance back, the glacier sparkles, as if Dad is winking at us.

The hurry is over. The hunger is over. The wondering when I'll find Dad is over too. The pain in my rib is my constant reminder that not all is well, but even so, the walk home is the first time on the whole trip that a few minutes pass and all I think about is the wind at my back, the tundra beneath my blistered feet, and absolutely nothing else.

I settle into the landscape.

The hike is long, but the hours pass more quickly with Ranger Collins and the other ranger in the lead and salami sandwiches in our bellies. They brought a tent for sleeping, too, and they used their satellite phone to leave a message for Mom that we were safe and okay.

The best moment happens when Sophie's in the lead. She yells, "Whoa!" and I'm afraid it's another grizzly. Then she chuckles.

"Just a silly ptarmigan," she says, and the brown bird scuttles across the trail — wearing its full set of summer feathers.

CHAPTER 34

The next day I look for the wolf when we get close to the McKinley River, but I don't see him. It's as if that wolf was a dream — a gift from another time and place.

The sun is high in the sky when we reach the river. Middle of the day is the worst time to cross, since the sun melts the glacier ice, which causes the river to rise. But the rangers don't look worried. And we're only a few hours from Wonder Lake.

The four of us link arms, and we cross all four strands easily. No wobbles. Maybe it's because after all this travel, the rivers have become part of us — and the cold isn't so cold anymore. Analyzing a river is about as tricky as analyzing why glaciers behave the way they do.

On the far bank, Sophie pulls off her backpack and rummages through to find something. She pulls out Dad's canoes. They've become old friends on this trip — faithful cups and constant reminders of Dad.

"So?" Sophie asks.

I nod in agreement. It's time.

Time to return them.

Sophie hands me one, and she keeps the other.

Together we walk to the edge of the water.

No words. Just simultaneous nods, and we drop the canoes — our improvised cups — into the McKinley for Dad's last race.

The boats zip down the river braid and arc around the left bend, where I washed up a few days ago. Then they fade into little brown specks bobbing on a silver current, until they disappear. Forever.

We walk for two more hours in complete silence — through the spruce forest, then the swamp, and finally across the rolling tundra path. It's a good silence. We might not be scaring away any bears, but with each step I feel closer to home.

When we're almost to the trail's end, Sophie says, "It's a miracle we made it."

"No, it's not," I say. "Dad taught us exactly what we needed to know."

CHAPTER 35

When the McKinley Bar Trail meets the campground road, the rangers turn right toward the station.

Sophie and I need to go left to get to the campground.

"Thank you," I say to them, even though *thank you* is not even close to enough.

"You're welcome. No more trouble today," Ranger Collins says, and winks. "I'll come check on you two in a few minutes. I'm going straight to the phone to call your mom again. Lily, your backpack is in the bear locker."

Ugh. We're going to be in big trouble with Mom. At the same time, I can't wait to tell her everything.

Sophie heads to the tent first, but I go straight to the bear locker. I can't wait for dry clean clothes and my warm sleeping bag.

I see her when I'm walking up the path to the locker.

"Mom!" I say, and run toward her.

It's really her.

She doesn't even look mad. We hug, and it's a real Mom hug. So real that I don't cringe at the rib pain. I'm here with Mom, and everything will be okay.

"I'm so sorry," I say.

"Sorry for what?" Mom asks.

"For disappearing off to Dad's mountain."

"You did what?" she says.

"Wait . . . Why did you come out here?" I ask.

"Home wasn't home without you two girls," Mom says.

That's when I get it. Mom doesn't have a clue about the adventures we've had. She must not have received the phone message from Ranger Collins. She came out here to find us because she couldn't stand to be away from us — and from the place that Dad loved.

We hug again, and I don't ever want it to end.

The three of us sit together at the picnic table and scarf down Mom's mac and cheese. Nothing in the world has ever tasted so delicious.

The mountain is in full view, but she's less huge now.

"Can you believe we were out there?" I say, pointing to the shimmery whiteness filling up the horizon.

"I'm glad I never knew," says Mom, but she's not angry. She has a tired twinkle in her eyes.

Mosquitoes buzz around us, but they can't ruin our dinner *or* this place with Mom.

"How was the river crossing?" Mom asks.

"You don't really want to know," says Sophie.

She chuckles. "Well, all that matters is we're all here now."

Here. Now. All of us. Well, not even close to all of us.

But being here with Mom is something.

"Did you wonder if we'd sneak to the mountain?" Sophie asks.

"You two are your father's daughters," says Mom. "If I'd thought much about it, I would have guessed so."

Mom's words, combined with her mac and cheese, warm me on the inside.

"But let's avoid glaciers for a little while, okay?"

"Deal," says Sophie.

"Absolutely," I add.

"My heart can't take any more," says Mom, and I know her words are true.

Mom pulls out the no-bake cheesecake, and we gobble up every last crumb.

"The most amazing thing about the Muldrow Glacier was the color of the snow and ice," I say. "I mean, it's not one color . . . it's always changing."

Mom smiles. "That's why your dad always had to go back there."

A raven circles overhead, and I wonder if it could be the same raven that dropped its feather before our trip to the mountain.

Mom continues: "I finally talked to John about Dad's fall. It was a clear Denali day with easy walking. The crevasse just opened up underneath him."

I swallow hard, and take the deepest breath I can muster.

"There was no way to see it coming," Mom says. "It was just one of those one-in-a-million chances. Pure unlucky."

"So that's why he didn't rope up?" I ask.

Mom nods slowly.

"Cheep, cheep, cheep." An arctic ground squirrel pops his head out of the ground and scans for predators.

This land is alive — harsh and changing — and it's right where I want to be.

I'm the first back to the tent for sleep. I fluff up my fleece jacket to be my pillow. Then I crawl into my own dry sleeping bag and settle in. No nightmare this time. When I close my eyes, I see Dad. He's sitting on the tundra eating peaches and gummy bears, sipping brandy, and playing one last game of Scrabble on earth.